I0846783

The Bored and the Cross

By: Greg Allen

The Bored and the Cross
Copyright © 2011 by Greg Allen.
All rights reserved.

This book is protected under the copyright laws of the United States of America. No part of this publication may be reproduced, stored in a retrieval system or transmitted in any way by any means, electronic, mechanical, photocopy, recording or otherwise without the prior permission of the author except as provided by USA copyright law.

Published by Builder of the Spirit Ministries
10465 West US Highway 136
Jamestown, Indiana 46147 USA
1.765.676.5014
www.builderofthespirit.org

ISBN 979-8-218-28122-9
Published in the United States of America

Book design copyright © 2011 by:
Builder of the Spirit Ministries
All rights reserved.

Other books by: **_Greg Allen_**

Builder of the Spirit
War of the Heart
Hear the Call

"Greg tells an excellent story. Great job! I could relate to so much of it."

Keith Wheeler ~ Founder of Keith Wheeler Ministries

Note: Since 1985, Keith has carried a 12' wooden cross in more than 130 countries on all seven continents while logging nearly 20,000 miles.

Dedication

This book is dedicated to my hero. Jesus, it's all about you!   I would also like to dedicate it to those who love Him and long for His presence. He may seem distant and difficult to find at times, but His companionship is always there. Obedience to His voice is the key.

Lord, you deserve all the glory, honor, and credit for this work. If you hadn't given the story-line to me that Saturday morning at the mailbox, in the twinkling of my mind's eye, this novel simply wouldn't be. You gave it when I stretched forth my hand and I thank you for that.

Prologue

The Bored and the Cross is a story of triumph and tragedy, one of loss and gain, of mistakes made and ones corrected. It's about a journey called life.

You'll follow Gregory Matthews along this path called life. He's just another man some say, or is he? Jeremiah 1:5 proclaims, *"Before I formed you in the womb I knew you, before you were born I set you apart; I appointed you as a prophet to the nations."* Gregory will never claim to be a prophet, but in the end, many will label him that.

Gregory is introduced to tragedy and loss the moment he takes a breath. He gains life, another loses. Through prayer, Gregory becomes set apart. But like many of us, he doesn't recognize God's hand until the beaten path lay beneath his feet.

It's been said that the rain falls on the just and the unjust and life tells us those words hold truth. Many blame God when the circumstances of life come, but what does that teach us about ourselves? Although the characters contained within these pages are fictional, they represent a cross section of society that act just like us.

Why do people do the things they do? That's the universal question, isn't it? One thing's for certain, we're all born with a defect called the sin nature and we will always struggle with its presence. Some find salvation at an early age, others later, but many never will.

From beginning to end, life's an adventure and along the way, Gregory will learn, as many do, that life starts with Him and it will end with Him. Come join this man, be a part of his life, and meet those who will shape Gregory's life on the path past boredom on the way to the cross.

The Gift

The snowflakes gently danced past her face. Only the frosted pane stood between her and the chill of their touch - Sarah remembered reading somewhere once that no two are ever the same. The scenery seemed quite poetic and humbling as she stared from her hospital room window at the first whispers of yet another winterly season born. Her heart filled with joy as the expectant mother gazed upon a small group of playful children while they sledded down a nearby snow covered bank. The youngsters seemed so happy, so innocent, so carefree.

A kind and gentle voice from behind broke her concentration upon a joyous, yet not so distant memory.

"Mrs. Matthews, are you OK?" The tall slender nurse softly asked.

"I'm fine. Just a little nervous though," Sarah was quick to add. "Thanks for asking … I know you're my day shift nurse, but what did you say your name was?"

"It's Emmy." The blonde RN replied.

Turning to the nurse, Sarah softly asked, "Emmy, has my husband called?"

"Not yet." was the twice-divorced professional's bold, yet somewhat uncaring reply.

The baby was going to be born soon and Sarah needed her Ed close by her side.

Emmy thought this conversation needed a little small talk in order to wave away some of the tension.

"Is this your first baby?" Emmy asked.

Sarah said, "Oh, yes; our first."

Emmy herself was the mother of three. "Do you know if it's gonna be a boy yet, or girl?"

"Oh yes, the Lord said it's gonna be a boy." answered Sarah, the hopeful mother to be.

Emmy stared at Sarah thinking - "Ok, whatever." But instead said, "Have you chosen a name for him?"

"Yes we have. His name is going to be Gregory Ian Matthews." Sarah cheerfully said.

"That's a beautiful name, Mrs. Matthews! Can I ask why the name Gregory?"

"I was looking through some books on baby names when I came across that. His name just jumped off the page at me. Gregory means watchman and I promised the Lord I would raise my son in His ways. I'm convinced he's going to be a powerful man of God, a watchman, one who the world will see!"

Emmy kept her opinion to herself, but thought, "That's nice, but I better get to work before the supervisor catches me."

"Well Mrs. Matthews, I better check your heart rate and the baby's." Emmy told Sarah.

Sarah sat down on the bed and after a few moments the nurse said, "Your heart rate is fine, Mrs. Matthews, and so is little Gregory's. Before I leave I'd better check on your progress, to see how

far along you really are. You can lay back and put
your knees up, please."

Sarah leaned back against the flat, lifelessly thin
pillow to gaze out the window yet again.

After Emmy had finished her examination, she
looked at Sarah with concern, trying to hide the
grim thought that rose within her. She knew
something was wrong, but didn't want to alarm her
patient with the trouble.

"Sarah, you're bleeding a little." The stern nurse
looked at her with concern. "I want you to try and
stay calm, I'll be right back." were her instructions
and gentle warning.

Sarah turned to the window to see the fall of the
sun - she blinked back the tears and whispered, "Oh,
Ed, I wish you were here!"

Emmy wasn't gone long until she returned with a
gurney and another nurse who seemed to beam with
excitement, yet it was all staged to cover her true
apparent fear.

"Sarah, Dr. Isaacs said we need to get you
prepped and ready for OR right away. Can you lie
down on this other bed for me? We'll get you ready
and then take you downstairs."

With a worried look upon her face, Sarah asked,
"Is my baby going to be OK?" The heart of the
5'2" brunette was now beginning to fill with fear.

Patting her patient's hand, the nurse said,
"Everything's going to be fine, Sarah." Emmy tried
to reassure her.

"Does my husband know?" Sarah anxiously
asked.

"I'll have the ladies downstairs give him a call, OK." The nurse was quick to answer.

"OK." Sarah said quietly, then she gave a lengthy gasp.

Emmy knew her patient's condition was serious but she never lost composure. She knew it was essential to keep Sarah calm but the nurse knew the doctor was in for a battle.

A short time later the phone rang at Ed Matthews's office. The secretary picked it up and said, "Performance, Inc. This is Donna speaking, may I help you, please?"

"This is the hospital calling, maam. Will you please tell Ed Matthews that his wife has been taken to the OR. We'd like for him to get here as soon as possible."

"I'll do it right now!" was the elderly secretary's reply.

The gentle voice on the other end of the line said, "Thank you, Donna, we'll be waiting, good-bye."

The secretary was instructed to never interrupt during a board meeting, but in her opinion this was an exception. She walked up to the board room door, knocked, then barged in.

Mr. Jones, the president, looked at his secretary in disgust then demanded, "What is it?"

She ignored her boss only to look over at Ed Matthews - Sarah's business minded spouse who she met through a mutual friend while at college.

"Mr. Matthews, the hospital called, Sir. They took your wife to the OR. They suggest you get there as soon as you can."

"Thank you, Donna." Ed replied. He turned to
his boss, Mr. Jones, then said, "Sir, I'd better go. I
think my wife needs me."

"Ed, you know this is a huge deal we're working
on. It means everything to us!"
Jones' tone was harsh. "If you leave, you'd better be
back that much earlier tomorrow, because life
doesn't stand still for you or I!"

Ed gathered his papers then his boss said loudly.
"Do you understand me?"

Ed answered, "Yes, Sir," and left the room.

As Ed walked to his car he kept thinking to
himself that everything was going to be fine. He'd
go to the hospital, spend some time with his wife,
and still be able to close that big deal on time. But
little did he know his life was about to dramatically
change. Life doesn't always go according to plan, as
he would soon see.

Along the way the 23-year-old Ed day-dreamed
of his true desire. His heart longed for that brand
new 1957 Chevy Bel-Air that was just sitting there
on the dealership showroom floor, waiting. If he
could only just close this deal he'd have those
wheels.

After he drove past the dealership Ed began to
talk to himself. You need to understand something
about Ed, he did so when he felt a nervous feeling
rise from within. He thought by doing so it would
give him the capability of a self-controlled mind.
"The salesman said it was going to be a classic
someday! As soon as I close that big deal that
baby's mine!" The concentration of his day-
dreaming mind was broken as he turned the corner,

then Ed said, "Oh, great, there's the hospital, I'm here, I hope she's fine!"

Ed parked the car and walked through the front door. As he walked through the vast complex of halls he began to realize the gravity of it all - he tried to convince himself that everything was going to be fine. He still knew in the back of his mind that his wife was pregnant, in the OR, and the risks were high.

He walked toward the Nurses Station while repeatedly whispering under his breath, "Everything's going to be fine. Everything's going to be fine."

An elderly black nurse said, "May I help you, Sir?" as she glared up at the clock upon the wall.

"Yes, I'm Ed Matthews. Someone here called and left word that my wife, Sarah, she's having a baby, was being sent to the OR and that I should get here as soon as possible."

"Mr. Matthews can you please have a seat in the waiting room. Dr. Isaacs will be in to see you in a few minutes." The nurse instructed him as she longed for just five more ticks of the clock, the end of her shift.

"Is everything alright?" Ed felt his voice rise. "Can I see my wife?"

Pointing her bony finger across the hall, the nurse said, "Sir, please! Have a seat in the waiting room. The doctor will be in shortly."

Ed walked through the waiting room door, and noticed he was the only one there. Ed, an overworked, slightly overweight, underpaid, workaholic tried to calm his mind. He thought he

would by grabbing a cup of Joe. They had "free"
coffee; Ed liked anything that was free. If he read
one those magazines on the table it might help him
pass the time and calm his nerves, but when he
reached for one Ed knocked the cup over. The
coffee ran all over the floor and as Ed reached for a
newspaper to clean up the mess he noticed Dr.
Isaacs walking down the hall towards him. Dr.
Isaacs was walking with his head down until he
caught sight of Ed through the glass of the waiting
room door.

As the kind doctor swung open the door, he said,
"Are you Ed Matthews?"

"Yes."

Ed shook the physician's hand and asked
worriedly, "What's happening?"

"I'm Dr. Isaacs… Mr. Matthews, I've been a
doctor for quite a number of years and this is never
easy. Lord, it's never easy."

His demeanor now serious and stern, Ed listened
to the doctor's every word with great concern.
"What are you trying to say?"

"Ed …"

"No, I don't think I'm ready!" Placing a hand
over his face, Ed began to pace.

 Dr. Issacs continued. "Ed, we saved your son
but we couldn't save your wife. She had severe
internal bleeding and we just couldn't stop it."

Ed stopped the pacing and collapsed into a chair.
"Oh … God … No! She's only 22!"

Dr. Issacs placed his hand on Ed's shoulder and
tears began to flow down the doctor's cheeks. "I'm

sorry Ed, I'm really sorry. We did everything we could."

Ed stared at the coffee, still wet upon the floor and said, "Did she say anything before she died?"

"I was with her when she died. She left us with such a peace upon her face, words cannot describe it. She told me she's always loved you, and that you were constantly in her prayers." The doctor's voice was soft and soothing. "She said God never gave up on you and neither did she. She said not to worry, she's with the heavenly Father and it will be a beautiful place there."

Ed finally looked up at Dr. Issacs and said, "That sounds just like somethin' she'd say. Are you a Christian too?"

The doctor smiled. "Yes I am."

Ed had grown up with hypocrites his entire life - the experience had galvanized his mind!   "Do you really believe that stuff, Doc?"

"Yes I do." The sincere doctor was quick to reply.

"I never saw the need!" said Ed. "Going to church, reading the Bible, believing in Jesus, stuff like that. It's all a bunch of lies!"

"It's gonna be my prayer you see the need! Ed, some things are just bigger than us all."
Dr. Issacs squeezed Ed's shoulder. "I suggest you go see your son, you'll need each other now."

After Dr. Issacs left Ed sat in the waiting room for quite some time before he could gather enough composure to walk to the elevator and push the "up" button. He said nothing during the ascent to the third floor - staring at the floor his mind consumed with the thought of God killing his wife. He loved her and God took her away. The doors opened. Ed took a deep breath and stepped out into a whole new world. The nursery viewing window was just around the corner.

Stepping up to the window, Ed's mind filled with the thought, "What in the world am I gonna do now since God has ruined my life?" The tag said, "Matthews - Boy." A son, his son. Ed stood and just stared. The game of life is never fair. Its circumstances had just dealt him a losing hand.

First Love

Time had passed slowly for Ed since the death of his wife, he did indeed miss her so, her warm gentle touch, the smell of her hair, and the way she would nervously use a finger to twirl those brown locks of hers. Once again, he found himself alone standing before his son to stare at him. The vivid memory of that day at the nursery room window flooded Ed's mind as he adjusted now 12-year-old Gregory's tie. He began to realize that his son was no longer a boy, but was becoming a man.

"Son, I'm proud of you!" Ed conveyed with great pride. "You're a fine lookin' young man!" With a smile and a wink, Ed asked, "Are you nervous about your first date?"

"A little." was Gregory's giddy reply.

"I can remember when your mom and I went out on our first date. God, I wish she could see you standing here." With a slight grin Ed shook his head from side to side. "You sure do look mighty fine!"

Looking in the mirror to do a quick hair align, Gregory asked, "Where'd you go, Dad?"

"What? … Oh, it was a 50's sock hop." Getting lost in the memory of his teenage days, Ed paused then hung his head and sighed, " That sure was a great day."

Ed raised his right eyebrow then grinned to say, "That night was our first kiss, son. God, I sure do miss those ruby red lips!"

It was his first date, but Gregory didn't dare verbalize the thought that raced through his mind. His dad could never know his ultimate concern - focus upon just this one beautiful girl. "What's a sock hop?" was Gregory's only inquiry.

"It's a dance similar to what you're going to. It was a place where kids went to have fun. Well, enough talk about me. Now, let's talk about you. After all, it's your big night! When were you planning on tellin' me your new girlfriend's name?"

Gregory pushed his father's hands out of the way and began adjusting his own tie. "She's not my girlfriend, Dad … If you must know, her name is Rebecca Stover. Everybody at school calls her Becky."

Dropping down on one knee, Ed grabbed the dramatics of center-stage. He glided his hand slowly upward in a semi-circle motion through the air as he said, "I can see the newspaper headline now. Gregory Matthews and Becky Stover … Broken Arrow, Oklahoma's own Jr. High spring dance king and queen crowned with royal thoroughfare."

Gregory thought, "Stop, that's embarrassing." but could only muster a lukewarm smile.

Ed stood back for a moment to gaze at Gregory. "I'm so proud of you, son." were his boastful words as he stared at the dual image of their reflection in the mirror.

"I know, Dad. But, if you really love me you'd stop working so much." That was Gregory's heart felt desire - a lonely cry - a pitiful plea.

"I know son. It's just that I promised myself after your mom died I would take care of you no matter what. I told her before we got married we would lack for nothing! I want all of the best things in life for you, Greg. And if that means working 24/7, so be it."

"I know, Dad! I've heard that lecture before, but that doesn't help me with my homework!"

Circumstances would never really change. Gregory just wanted a dependable father - Ed thought he was being one.

"Well, we better get going. We'd better not be late. Becky's probably waitin' on us." was Ed's hurried Saturday evening plea.

Ed picked up Becky at her home then dropped the couple off at the Jr. High. It would be their first date, but it was just the beginning of the destiny of God's beautiful hand upon both their lives.

Time was quick to pass, days became weeks, weeks became months, and months turned into years. Gregory and his dad grew farther apart but he and Becky grew closer. Their yearbook read like a romance novel - he a track star, she the head cheerleader. Time for high school graduation drew near.

One day after school the couple's conversation got quite heated. There was no doubt in each of their minds there was love for each other, fate had seen to that at the first Jr. High dance, but Becky had always thought there was just something a little missing.

"Greg, remember what we talked about? I mean, have you given it any more thought about Oral Roberts? I've heard it's a great school!"

A minor outburst of anger was Gregory's frustrated cry. "Becky, that's all you talk about!"

Becky ran her hand over Gregory's chest and tilted her head over on his side then said, "I just think it would be groovy to spend our lives together as missionaries, don't you?"

Practice was over and Gregory waited for the line of Jocks to file by. Trying to defuse the moment, Gregory sat erect upon the bench they were sitting on in the school courtyard and said, "Beck, I did what you told me to do last Sunday. I went to church with you like ya wanted. I went down front and repeated that prayer the minister said. You told me that I got saved, what more is it you want? I know graduation's only a few weeks away, but to be honest, I don't really know what I want."

"I see!" was Becky's brisk response as she sat up to give her boyfriend a real stern stare. "I know what God's calling me to do … If you don't go to Oral Roberts with me … I don't see how our relationship can survive."

Gregory shouted out, "Oh, come on … just because you think you have to preach to all those jungle natives that doesn't mean I have to!"

Gregory's concern soon heightened with Becky's every word spoken. "If you really love me

Greg, you'll spend your life with me, no matter where that journey may take us."

Standing to stare down at his girlfriend, Gregory's face became inflamed – the veins in his forehead now protruded with anger. "That's some heavy stuff, Beck!" Pointing his finger at her, Gregory quickly said, "My dad warned me about you and your family. He said that you were a bunch of Christian losers, but I didn't believe him. He said you were gonna throw your life away just like my mom did." Gregory's tone filled with rage, his volume got louder and louder. "He calls you guys Jesus Freaks!"

Gregory's attitude then quickly turned to that of sarcastic joking. "He said people that wanna be ministers love telling people what to do. They are always begging for money because it's a lousy paying job, if you can call it a job! They try to tell everybody else how to live their lives when they can't even manage their own." Gregory was quick to switch back to that of anger. "Now you're telling me how to run mine! Dad was right, you're all a bunch of religious fruitcakes. I don't wanna hear anymore, I'm gone. I'm history!"

Shocked and surprised, Becky stood and watched her boyfriend walk out of her life. "Greg!" she called after him.

Angry and now full of resentment, Gregory turned back around to yell at her, "That's it, we're finished - bye!"

Both thought that was the end of their relationship, but was it? God wasn't quite finished yet - He was just starting to draw the plan. It was only just the beginning of a journey, one that would eventually lead to the foot of the *Cross.*

High school graduation finally came.

The graduation ceremony had ended earlier and all the relatives left Ed's house after the party. That's because the cake and punch were all gone and none of the family members were much of a social bunch. Then Ed decided it was time to have a serious talk with his son.

"Son, I know you're *Bored* and you don't know what you wanna do with your life, but don't you think it's time to stop playing around! Now, I've given this decision a lot of thought."

Gregory sat on the couch, looked up at his dad and said, "What are you tryin' to say?"

Ed paced the floor in front of his son then said, "Greg, I want you to go to Harvard."

Gregory nodded his head several times up and down then rolled his eyes while thinking to himself, "I've heard that one a thousand times!"

Pointing his finger at his son, Ed said, "Listen, here's the deal. Either you're goin' to Harvard like I did, or you're gonna hit the street!"

Sitting erect and just boiling with revolt, Gregory said, "What if I don't wanna go to Harvard? What if I don't wanna be a stockbroker like you were?"

Rage then began to wage war upon the heart of the father. "Listen to me you little punk! Wall street has been good to us!"

Anger now descended upon the son and Gregory stood to stare down into the eyes of his father. "You mean it's been good to you, Dad! You've never been home long enough from the office or away from that secretary of yours to understand that one … have you?"

Fury boiled over then Ed slapped Gregory's face.

Gregory rubbed his cheek and glared at his dad. "I'm gone!" He said.

"Where you goin' now, boy?"

Ed grabbed the arm of his son and Gregory was quick to jerk it away.

"Away from you!"

"If you walk out that door you're never comin' back, you understand me?" was Ed's final plea.

Gregory said, "Perfectly!" with a disgusted tone.

Gregory turned to leave then turned back to his dad. "Becky was right about you all along, old man! Money's your god."

Gregory walked into his bedroom, packed a bag, then walked out of his father's life. Ed didn't even say good-bye.

Gregory walked around town for quite some time just trying to think of what to do. As he was walking he noticed that he passed the street that Becky lived on. It was a bold thought that came to him, but he decided to give it a shot.

Gregory walked up to Becky's door and knocked. His ex-girlfriend answered the door. "I'm surprised to see you," she said. "Would you like to come in?"

Gregory shook his head, walked over to the edge of the porch and threw his bag to the ground. As he began to sit down, Gregory said, "My life's over!"

Becky could only stare through the screen as the teen hung his head on his knees.

Becky's heart quickly filled with forgiveness and compassion, she opened the screen door and walked across the porch to also sit on the front steps. When Becky sat down beside him, she put her arm around Gregory then whispered in his ear, "No, it's not, it's only just the beginning!"

They talked for what seemed like hours. He told her of his fight with his dad and how he could never go back.

"Becky, I've been a jerk!" That was Gregory's honest and heartfelt cry.

"Yes, you have." Becky said with a slight smile.

Turning his head to the side to look Becky straight in the eye, Gregory said, "Can you ever forgive me?"

With a tear beginning to well up, Becky said, "I already did. Just because we didn't see eye to eye, that doesn't mean I ever stopped loving you."

As they both gazed up into the night's star covered sky, Gregory asked, "Are you still up for Oral Roberts? … I don't know what we'll do for money though."

Becky reached over to give Gregory a slight peck on the cheek then said, "We'll worry about that later, OK. At least we'll be together, you and me."

Gregory leaned back, placed his hands behind his head, and began to stare upon the heavens. "Ok … just you and me."

Betrayal

That next morning found Gregory rising from the Stover's couch - it was truly the dawn of a new day. Becky and Gregory had the entire day planned out. Together they were going to grab a bite of breakfast and then make the short drive to Oral Roberts University in Tulsa. That day would be the start of their new life together as Becky had envisioned it, but the path of life isn't always a straight one, it's full of twists and turns and both would soon see that.

You see, that day was enrollment day at ORU. It was a wonderful day for Becky. Her hopes, dreams, and prayers were finally answered, or so she thought. On the other hand, Gregory felt trapped. He cared for Becky but it simply wasn't the deep heart felt love that she had for him. He hid his feelings pretty well. The true desire of his heart wasn't to attend that university at all, but in his mind he reasoned that he had no choice at all. He couldn't go home again, and although Becky kept saying it was a tremendous opportunity they had, Gregory didn't think so but just simply went along.

As they stood in line to enroll the excitement and enthusiasm of the day began to boil. Becky's spirit filled with an unspeakable joy, it was like nothing she'd ever experienced before.

Gregory now stood to tower over Becky, he was 5' 10" tall. She a mere 5' 4". Both were now adults, no longer just kids. As Gregory stared at his girlfriend he couldn't help but remember back upon their childhood days, of the day he first saw her. Gregory's first impression back then was to ask a friend, "Hey, who's that beautiful new blonde with the braces?"

Becky's parents had moved to Oklahoma from the deep south when she was just eight. Her father, a painter, had moved in hopes of finding work and a better life. Becky was their only child, a miracle, considering Mrs. Stover had lost four babies before. Becky was now a full figured girl and other guys were quick to notice – although Gregory didn't really seem to mind all those peering eyes. You might say he was still just a confused young boy, now trapped in a man's body.

Rubbing her hand on Gregory's back, Becky said, "Oh, Greg. This is so groovy! Me and you together like this."

 Gregory said, "Yeah." as he tried to sound excited, even though he wasn't.

The course of the day was demanding but they got through it and eventually it came time to settle into their new environment, the dorm rooms. Greg and Becky began to realize that their savings would only get them so far in their quest for academic excellence. They knew that part-time jobs were inevitable, the money they had wouldn't go far. As they stood outside the girls dorm, the hour became late. Their conversation ofemployment opportunities and their future together came to an end with a passionate kiss at the gate.

Greg kissed her for what seemed like an eternity. In her heart, she would have given anything to bottle that moment. In Becky's mind this was the best day of her life, she was truly happy for the longing of her heart had been truly fulfilled.

Gregory gazed into her deep blue eyes as he stroked her long blonde hair. "Good night, Beck."

Becky hugged Gregory's tall 150 pound frame. "Night, I love you."

"Yeah, me too." was Gregory's pathetic reply.

Neither Becky or Gregory enjoyed living in the dorms, but they knew it was going to be a way of life for the next few years. When living in a dorm, one can have quite unusual roommates. Becky and Gregory were no exception. Becky's roommate was Helen Smith from Warm Springs, Georgia. Becky thought Helen was a sweet girl, but she was quite the introvert. Helen had virtually no friends. When she wasn't in class she spent the rest of her time in their room listening to her Beach Boys record collection. Becky had repeatedly told her to get out more, but that seemed to fall on deaf ears. Becky was simply too embarrassed to invite Gregory to her room because Helen always chose to wear a robe, a mud pack, and curlers in her hair.

Gregory had quite an unusual roommate, too. His roommate was Elvis Jones from Smithville, Mississippi. Elvis was a quiet young black man who loved to play the guitar, but he really wasn't very good at it. He couldn't carry a tune in a jar. Elvis would frequently tell Gregory that the Word says make a joyful noise and he was faithful to give it his best shot. Elvis had a record collection, too. He had every hit the King of Rock and Roll ever produced. Gregory thought to himself, "This is gonna be a long four years!"

Classes didn't start for a couple weeks so the couple thought it appropriate to start job hunting. Gregory got lucky. He was hired on the spot at the local IGA grocery, as a stock clerk. He attributed his success in landing the job to his previous experience at the Broken Arrow A & P Super Mart where during high school he was a bagger. But never once did he give God any of the credit for finding a good job so fast.

On the other hand, Becky wasn't quite so lucky. She made several attempts to land a job and experienced the frustration of filling out a lot of applications. She finally got an opportunity for employment and was accepted as a night-shift waitress at one of the local steakhouses. It was hard work and thankless. The pay was a dollar an hour and if she was lucky she might get a tip or two.

It was a blessing that both had transportation but neither one of their cars was much to brag about. Gregory owned a 1972 Chevy Nova, it didn't have a bit of rust but it had 183,000 miles on it. Becky owned a 1973 Ford Pinto that had low mileage but she always called it, "A real rust bucket."

The next four years would truly be a test of their faith and the lop-sided love they had. Becky had a strong personality and a faith in God to match while Gregory had a different kind of faith. Gregory believed what the world believed - "Seeing is the only real truth." In Becky's opinion, that wasn't faith at all. She was convinced the Bible meant truth.

From the time she was a little girl Becky's mother told her to take a scripture and stand on it, she remembered that. Her favorite verse was 2 Corinthians 5:7. "We live by faith, not by sight." Becky would come to realize that her level of faith in Christ wasn't something that was transferable to another. The harder she tried to develop the character of Christ in Gregory, the colder and more distant he slid from God.

The first year at ORU passed rather quickly for the couple, Becky's parents would visit quite often. They were a rock of encouragement when it came to giving her a phone call or sending a card for that special occasion. That simply wasn't the case for Gregory. His dad was a man of his word. After he stated, "Greg, you walk out that door you walk out of my life" it became sealed in concrete when the door shut. Although Ed lived only a few miles away he never made an attempt to contact his son.

The first year found the couple spending most of their spare time together. Their savings allowed them to work less hours on the job so they could spend more time together. The second year was pretty much like the first but things started to change in the third. Their savings ran out and both were forced to work daily. The routine of going to school all day and working most of the night began to tear away at their relationship. They began to see less of each other and when that special occasion did arise Gregory would quite often say, "I'm bored with all this!" then usually say, "I'll pass, maybe some other time."

Although Becky knew full well what she wanted to be, Gregory wasn't quite so sure and seemed to just struggle through life. People from work constantly told Gregory he was throwing his life away and that he would live a life of poverty if he became a minister. Those thoughts began to frequently flood his mind and one day he acted upon them.

Gregory knew a young man by the name of James who worked for a Wall Street broker. He lived in New York City and had become close friends with Gregory over the past couple of years. James met Gregory through a rather unique set of circumstances. James's father was a broker just like Gregory's was. Both fathers used to work together years ago, but when Sarah died Ed pulled up stakes to move as far away from up state New York as he could. He eventually planted roots in, of all places, Oklahoma, the Sooner State. The boys developed a friendly relationship with each other in their childhood and rebuilt it a decade later thanks to a few letters and a phone call now and then.

Gregory woke up that Sunday morning with a different agenda in mind. You see, Oral Roberts University always conducted chapel services on Sunday morning for the students and Gregory decided not to go that day. He made up his mind that his Bible college career was over. He knew it would be a shot in the dark but he would give it the old college try. Gregory would call his friend James in New York.

The voice on the other end of the line said, "Hello."

"James, it's Greg."

"Oh, hi!" was James's reply.

"I really need to talk to you." Gregory said with concern.

James asked, "What's on your mind?" .

"I've decided to leave ORU."

"Why?"

"To be honest, I'm bored with the lifestyle. I don't see me and Becky goin' in the same direction anymore. I don't know why I ever enrolled in this school in the first place. Felt like I had no choice, I guess that's why."

James asked, "What are you going to do?"

"Well, that's why I'm calling you. I got a proposal."

"Go ahead … I'm listening."

"I was thinking that I could come and stay with you until I get on my feet." was Gregory's begging plea.

"And do what?" was James's stern, questioning concern.

"I was thinking that I could work to get my trading license and then when I get on my feet I could get me a place. You know that I know the ropes and maybe you can pull a few strings."

"Are you sure that's what you wanna do?" James began to reason.

"Yeah, I've been thinkin' about it for a long time." Gregory replied.

"I don't care if you come." James said, "Have you told Becky yet?"

"No. That's goin' be the hard part."

James asked, "You got money to get here?"

Unsure of how a new roommate might work, James said, "Yeah, I'll see you next week, OK?"

"Yeah, next week."

Gregory said, "Thanks … I owe ya, bye."

James hung up the phone shortly after saying, "Good -bye."

Gregory knew his car wouldn't make it to New York so he decided to take his roommate, Elvis, up on his offer to purchase the car for a hundred bucks. Gregory sold the car to purchase a bus ticket and only had a couple hours left before the bus would depart.

He was all packed and ready to go, but couldn't handle a face to face confrontation so the coward decided to give Becky a call. He knew it was gonna be one of the hardest phone calls he'd ever make in his life, so he sat back, dialed the number, and rolled the dice.

Becky's sweet voice answered after just one ring, "Hello."

"Becky?" was Gregory's nervous reply.

"Yes."

Gregory said, "It's me."

"Oh, hi." Becky replied.

"Hi, Becky. I" … Gregory hesitated. "I don't know how to say this."

"Say what?" Becky asked.

"I'm leaving school." was the bombshell that Gregory now dropped in the lap of his unsuspecting girlfriend.

"What?" Becky couldn't believe she'd heard him right.

"I'm leaving." Gregory repeated.

In shock, Becky said, "Why?"

"Well, it's a number of things." Gregory reasoned.

"Like what?" Becky wanted to know.

"Well, first of all, I didn't really want to come to this school in the first place."

"But, I thought you wanted to come here for us, to be together?"

"Not really. The reason why I came was because I felt like I had no other choice when my dad kicked me out. I only stayed as long as I did because I thought you wanted me to. I've never really been happy here at all."

There was dead silence on Becky's end of the line.

"I'm moving in with a friend in New York. I'm gonna pursue my broker's license. Becky, this Christian life of poverty is your idea, not mine."

Although Gregory couldn't hear it or see it, tears were welling up in Becky's eyes.

"Becky, I need to get a couple things off my chest … You know the time I went down front at your church and repeated what your pastor said."

"Yes." was Becky's reply.

"I didn't really ask Jesus to come into my heart at all."

"What?" another shocking blow.

"What I'm trying to say is, I've never really been saved."

"But you said the sinner's prayer." Becky reasoned.

"I know what I said, but I didn't really mean it, not a word. I went down there so you would stop bugging me."

Becky said, "Oh, my God," as the tears began to flow.

"Becky, this is the end of our relationship. I thought I could work my way into loving you but it simply isn't working out. What I'm trying to say is, I don't think I have ever really loved you."

"You've got your mind made up?" Becky questioned quietly.

Gregory said, "Yes … yes … I have."

"I'm sorry to hear that, but before you leave me I've got somethin' to say. I have always been honest with you and it appears that you haven't been honest with me. I love you. I have loved you since the first time I laid eyes on you, that won't go away. This is going to hurt, but I forgive you for the deception and wish you the best. I hope you find what you're looking for out there."

"I'm sorry it has to end this way." Gregory added.

Her dreams, visions, now crumbling down around her, Becky said, " Yeah … me too."

"Bye, Beck."

"Bye …"

Gregory was about to embark on a different path through life. It was just the beginning for what God had in store, but Becky's hopes and dreams had now become shattered. She laid on her bed and filled her

pillow with tears as she tried to accomplish an
impossible task – one of crying herself to sleep.

City Lights

Elvis gave Gregory a ride to the bus terminal and helped him on his way.

"Greg, I hope you know what you're doing?"

"Yeah … me too."

"Thanks for being my friend, roomy."

"You too."

"Good luck, see ya later hounddog!"

"Bye … get out of here!"

The two shook hands and departed. As Gregory waited for his bus to arrive he began having second thoughts. He was clearly a young man with a torn mind. He convinced himself that New York was the thing to do and it was time to move on and not look back.

The bus arrived at the terminal and the call soon came to load the passenger luggage. As Gregory was loading his bag in the storage compartment of the bus the driver asked him where he was headed. His answer was, "I'm headed for fame and fortune."

The bus rolled out of the terminal and Gregory's new adventure had begun. It didn't seem like a long trip, but on the other hand Gregory couldn't tell, he slept most of the way.

Gregory's bus finally made it to New York. He was in awe of the city. He thought to himself, "The lights … look at all the lights." It reminded him of the early days of his childhood.

Gregory's father had a degree in finance from Harvard and he decided it would be best for him and Gregory to move to New York after his wife died. Ed's stockbroker days on Wall Street lasted roughly ten years when he decided to move to Broken Arrow. You might say Ed had a restless spirit. He always told Gregory that he made enough money on Wall Street to live comfortably and he didn't want his son exposed to the danger and corruption of the city.

After Gregory grabbed his bag he walked from the terminal to the street and hailed a cab. Once inside he said, "Central park, please." That was Gregory's favorite place to go as a boy. He sat on a bench for what seemed like hours and just watched. His childhood memories were coming back to him. He remembered the runners, the people walking their dogs, and most of all, the lovers who enjoyed each other's company on the blankets that were spread out on the ground.

In the quiet of his thoughts he began to argue with his conscience. His mind was literally at war. One thought would say that he walked away from a beautiful gal that absolutely loved him and another would say who needs her. Although Gregory had studied at ORU he didn't really follow the principles that the school had taught. He thought that praying or reading the Bible was boring. While in school it was of little or no interest to him. The only time he would pray or talk to God was when he was in trouble or needed something. You might say that his conscience was really bothering him. It was about that time he decided enough was enough.

He yelled, "God, I know what I'm doing! Leave me alone!"

Gregory walked over to a pay phone and called his friend James.

"Hello."

"Hey, I'm in Central Park. Can you come and pick me up?"

"What are you doing there?"

"Oh, it's a long story."

"Ok, I'll be there in a few minutes."

"Alright, see ya then."

James picked Gregory up and they went back to his apartment. As Gregory was getting settled in James mentioned that he had set up an interview with his boss for Greg on the following Monday.

"It's a page job." James said. "But it's a start. I figure you can work your way up the ranks. What do you think?"

"Sounds good. Hey, I really appreciate all this."

"No problem. Hey, I better get some sleep. I got to get up early in the morning for work."

"Ok, night."

Gregory watched some television and eventually retired for the evening himself.

Gregory spent the next few days getting a feel for the city, a feel for Wall Street, and to just shop for a new wardrobe at his favorite store, Macy's.

"Greg! Get up man, it's Monday. It's your big day."

"What time is it?"

"It's six A.M."

"Oh great, I can see that this is going to take some getting used too."

"Good morning to you, too. You nervous?"

"A little."

"You'll be fine! Got to go, see ya tonight."

"Bye."

After Gregory had taken a shower he put on his brand new three piece suit and tie. As he stared in the mirror to get dressed, he began to think of ORU and Becky. He was quite literally at war with his thoughts. He had convinced himself that her lifestyle was boring. That's all she wanted to talk about was Jesus, but he really knew down deep that she loved him and he was a jerk for treating her the way he did. As he stared in the mirror it gave him a chance to view what he had become. He thought to himself, "I'm becoming the exact same thing that I hated in my dad." He shook his head to the side as if to shake that thought off and said out loud, "It's time to land that job!"

Gregory arrived at the brokerage firm with ten minutes to spare. While he was waiting in the lobby he thought to himself, "The traffic in this city is murder!"

The receptionist interrupted his thoughts.

"Mr. Matthews, Mr. Lemon will see you now."

"Thank you."

He was ushered into Mr. Lemon's office.

"So … you're Ed's boy?"

Mr. Lemon stood up and shook Gregory's hand.

"Yes, sir!"

"Have a seat, son. Me and your dad go back a long ways. How's he doin' anyway?"

"Fine. He's doing fine."

"Well, to be honest with you it's just a page job on the floor that pays three hundred a week, but it's yours if you want it."

"I'll take it!"

"OK then. You can start tomorrow. See my secretary on the way out. And oh, by the way, I'm goin' be keepin' my eye on you."

"Thank you, Sir!"

"Call me Jim. That's what my friends call me."

"OK, thank you, Jim."

Gregory shook hands with his new boss and walked into what he thought would be a promising new life. As soon as he got back to James' apartment he gave him a call at work.

"Lemon, Lemon and Ruffin. James speaking."

"Hey!   I got the job."

"Great! We'll go out and celebrate tonight. I know this really cool place. It's called Studio 54."

"Sounds good, see ya."

Later on that evening, while riding in the cab to Studio 54, the conversation between James and Gregory got quite personal.

As both men stared out the cab's window at the lights of the city James asked, "Did you ever do it with Becky?"

Gregory answered angrily, "What kind of question is that?"

"Well, did ya?"

"NO!"

"Why not?"

"Shut-up, why ya askin' that?"

"Have you ever been to a night club before?"

"NO!"

"What do you think Studio 54 is?"

"I don't know! If ya ever ask a question like that again I'll knock your teeth out! Understand?"

"Sorry!"

The cab driver pulled over to the side and yelled. "You're here. That'll be seventeen fifty."

As James paid the driver Gregory asked, "What is this place?"

"It's Sex, Drugs and Rock and Roll that's what it is!"

"I see!"

Immediately a thought flashed through Gregory's mind. A professor at ORU once told him that sin will take you farther than you plan to go and keep you longer than you want to stay.

"Greg, let's go!"

Gregory shook off the thought and said, "OK."

They walked in and found a table in the corner. Gregory thought to himself, "This place is wild."

The waiter said, "Can I take your order?"

James told the waiter, "We'll take two drafts. One for me and my friend."

Gregory looked at James and told him, "I've never drank before."

"Well there's a first time for everything."

The music was loud and the place was dark but a certain young lady who was sitting a couple of tables over caught Gregory's eye.

"Hey, James. Who's that?"

James looked where Gregory was looking.

"You like her?"

"She's beautiful!"

"That's Angela Buttman. Her dad's Jimmy Buttman."

"Who?"

"You've never heard of Jimmy Buttman?" James looked amazed.

"No, I can't say I have."

"He owns just about half of Manhatten, and he's also one of our clients. If you like what you see I'll introduce ya to her. She's a rich party girl!"

"Ok … I like!"

James and Gregory walked up to Angela's table where she was sitting with a friend.

"Hi, I'm James and this is Greg."

"Hi, boys! I'm Angela and this is my friend Tina."

James looked at Tina and asked her to dance.

"Sure." As Tina and James were walking away she said, "See you two later."

Gregory looked at Angela and he was stunned by her beauty.

Angela said, "Are you going to just stand there and stare or are you going to have a seat?"

"Oh … sorry."

He pulled over Tina's chair and sat down.

"My name's Gregory."

"Gregory what?"

"Gregory Matthews. My friends call me Greg."

"Hi, Greg." She purred.

"Hi."

Gregory thought, "This is going to be a great night!" Thoughts of being with her danced round about his head. Little did he know this was going to

be just the beginning of what would be a very
troublesome relationship between the two.

The Seductress

James and Gregory became quite drunk that evening. The two finally made it home and as they staggered up the stairs with their arms around each other they both looked at each other and simultaneously said, "Thank God for taxi cabs!"

Both young men had severe hang-overs the following morning. As they sat at the kitchen table pouring coffee down their throats, Gregory said something quite interesting, yet, humorous.

"You know something James?"

"What?"

"We got a sayin' back in Oklahoma."

"And what might that be?"

"If yer gonna run with the big dogs, ya better get out from under the porch."

"What?"

"Oh, never mind."

"What ever!"

Gregory was indeed captivated by Angela's beauty, but he knew he was out classed.

"Do you think Angela would go out with me?"

James burst out in laughter.

"What's so funny?"

"You! Maybe in another life."

They both laughed at that.

"That's it!" Gregory suddenly said.

"What's it?"

"I'm going to start taking night classes so I can finish my degree."

"In what?

"Finance."

"How are ya gonna to do that? Oh, listen to me. I'm starting to talk like you. Besides, you been studying God for the last three years. Or should I say God's been studying you."

"That's low man." Gregory grinned. "I'll just transfer my credits. It may take a little longer, but that's what I'll have to do to have Angela."

"Right!" James wasn't convinced.

Gregory enrolled in night classes at the local university the following week, and eighteen months later he had that cherished degree. His major was in finance with a minor in religious studies. (Transferred from ORU) Things began looking up for Gregory after he got that diploma. He was offered an apprentice broker position at the firm, which he accepted. Using the bonuses he earned, it didn't take him long to pay off his student loan and move up the corporate ladder. In a short period of time he even earned that coveted title of broker, but that wasn't really of importance to him. His mind was overwhelmingly consumed with the thoughts of having Angela, and those thoughts would soon be realized.

It was just another day at the water cooler at work, or was it? As Gregory bent over for a drink he felt someone brush against him. As he tilted his head to the side to see who it was, his reaction became not one of anger, but of pleasant surprise.

"Hi, Angela! What brings you down here?"

"You." She smiled and Greg's stomach flipped.

"Me?"

"I heard you made broker and I'd like to take you out for a drink."

"Now?"

"Yeah, my dad's in your boss's office right now telling him to give you the day off."

She then began to play with his silk tie.

"He is?"

"Yes … he is. See what money can do? I love it, Greg, its power! Are you ready?"

"Well, if it's all right with my boss, then I guess I am."

As Angela and Gregory took the elevator ride down and made their way to the street his mind began to fill with lustful thoughts. Angela's mind was also becoming filled with lustful thoughts. As they waited to hail a cab, both became consumed with the thought of having each other.

"Greg, have you ever been to *Down and Dirty*?"

"What's that?"

"It's a night club, silly."

"Sorry, I can't say I have."

"Would you like to try it?"

"Sure."

In the back of his mind he despised night clubs and the bar scene, but Gregory was willing to sacrifice what little morals remained in order to have her.

"Here we are." The cab driver said. "Down and Dirty. That'll be $13.75."

Gregory paid him.

"Thanks driver, keep the change."

Gregory and Angela sat at a table for two in a dark corner of the bar. They said little to each other at first, but after the second or third drink Angela decided to make her move. While staring passionately into his eyes she slid her hand over his. Angela began to gently rub her fingers up and down the back of Gregory's hand. His mind began to race as they looked into each others eyes. Their lips began to get closer and closer until Gregory could not resist any longer and he kissed her. The two kissed throughout the night, danced, and proceeded to get quite drunk.

Angela finally asked the question they were both thinking.

"Greg, would you like to go to my place?"

Gregory didn't hesitate.

"I'll call a cab."

They arrived at Angela's apartment building and made their way past the doorman and up the stairs.

"Angela, I'm pretty drunk."

"I know!   You know I can't send you home like this. You'll have to stay the night."

"OK."

It was all that Gregory could do to get to the couch. He fell over the arm of the couch face first into the cushions.

She grinned and said, "I'll fix us a drink. Click the remote and start the fireplace up."

It was quite obvious what the two had in mind, and it didn't take long for their bodies to become intertwined with each other.

Gregory awoke the next morning to find that Angela had left. Only the maid remained, and she just smiled while dusting the furniture. Gregory jumped out of bed and ran to the bathroom where his clothes were hanging. Only a sheet covered his naked body.

Gregory returned home to find his roommate waiting.

"Where have you been? I have been worried sick!   At least you could have called."

"I spent the night at Angela's."

"Did you do her?"

"Shut up!"

"Did ya?"

"I was so drunk I don't remember much of anything. I do remember waking up in her bed naked and the maid laughing at me, but that's about it."

"You don't love her or anything, do you? Take my word for it. You just got lucky, my friend! She's the type of woman that breaks hearts for a living."

"I don't know, maybe you're right."

 Over the course of the next few weeks Gregory would call Angela, but she never returned the calls he placed with her answering service. Roughly six weeks later Gregory got a return phone call from Angela, but it wasn't quite what he expected.

"Greg, I have some bad news."

"Why haven't you returned my calls?"

"I haven't got time for that, listen to me. I'm pregnant! My father is threatening to cut off the money if I don't marry the baby's father."

"Who's baby is it?"

"It's yours!"

"Are you sure?"

"Yes!"

"Are you absolutely sure?"

"Yes!"

"Well, what do you want to do?"

"Will you marry me?"

"What about an abortion?"

"My father said that's not an option either. If I kill his grandchild, he will cut me off."

"Oh Angela … I don't think I can handle all this!"

"That's not all. My father asked who the father was. I told him you were. He said, if that guy doesn't marry you and give that baby a family he'll see to it that you never work on Wall Street again."

"Can he do that?"

"Yes, I'm sure he can."

"Angela, do you really think we should get married?"

"I don't see how we have much of a choice."

"To be honest with you, neither do I. I guess we set a date."

Till Sin Do Us Part

Angela was five months pregnant when Halloween came, and the wedding was finally at hand.

"Angela, of all days, why did you pick Halloween?" Gregory asked. "Nobody gets married on Halloween!"

"That's what I want, and that's what I'll get!   Is that inconvenient for you? Inconvenience is my middle name, pal. While we're on the subject, how'd you like throwing up every morning and looking in the mirror at a belly like this one!" She lifted her blouse and grabbed her stomach. "I'm sick of this thing already! I can't live like I wanna live!"

"Do you realize what you're saying?"

"Yeah!"

"Angela, if I felt like there was a way out of this I would take it."

"You and me both, pal!"

Gregory was beginning to see a side of Angela that he never experienced before. Angela's happiness with her pregnancy wasn't materializing. Seeds of jealousy, bitterness, and resentment were beginning to take root in her.

Mr. Buttman interrupted them.

"The guests are all seated and the preacher is ready, sweetheart."

"Dad, are you sure you won't change your mind about this wedding?"

"Angela, don't start! You're going marry to him and give that baby a home. End of story! Got me?"

"Yes, Daddy."

As the couple were standing for the vows, both their minds were far from the events at hand. Both felt trapped by life's circumstance. The thought raced through Gregory's mind, "How is this going to turn out?" Only time would tell.

"Humm!" The preacher said.

The couple said sorry simultaneously.

"Angela, do you take this man for your husband?"

"Yeah."

"Ok then. So, Gregory, do you take this woman for your wife?"

"Yeah."

"Ok then, I now pronounce you man and wife. You may kiss the bride."

They were showered with birdseed on their way out of the church. The couple packed their bags that night and flew to Hawaii for a honeymoon. Angela hated every minute of it.

"It's our first day here. Beautiful place, don't you think?"

They could see the ocean from their room.

"It would be, if I didn't look like a cow and I didn't have to pack a circus tent instead of a bikini."

"Will you stop being so negative?"

"What's it to you? Daddy's paying for everything anyway, you ain't out nothin'."

The honeymoon lasted a little over a week and Gregory was beginning to have second thoughts about his decision to marry Angela.

The big day came. March 3rd, 1984. A day of remembrance, or was it? Or was it just another day that Angela desired to forget about? Cloudy, rainy and cold were the New York skies that day.

"Mr. Matthews?"

"Yes."

"Hi, I'm Dr. Lowe. I just wanted to stop by and tell you that you have a beautiful eight pound daughter, sir."

"Everything OK?"

"Mother and baby are doing just fine. You can go see them now."

As Gregory approached the room he noticed that the nurses, for some reason, were leaving the room in a hurry, he was welcomed into the room by a barrage of complaints from Angela.

"It's about time!"

"Where are the nurses going in such a hurry?"

"I threw them out!"

"Why?"

"They're stupid and can't get anything right!"

"Oh, I see. They're not perfect like you are."

"Shut-up!"

"What's wrong with this picture? You would think you'd be happy? You just gave birth to our daughter."

"I just went through 20 hours of labor, jack! Try pushing a watermelon out your crotch and see how you like it!"

"The nurse wants to know the baby's name so she can fill out the birth certificate. What name did you decide on for a girl?"

"How about 'L'."

"L"? What kind of name is that?"

"L", Yeah, that's right, "L." … "L" … for loser!"

"You're not going to name her that!"

"I'll name her anything I please!"

"Used to getting your way about everything, aren't ya?"

"Yeah!"

"You make me sick! I'm goin' get a drink. I'm out of here!"

As Gregory walked out of the hospital room, Angela yelled, "L Matthews it is!"

As Gregory rode the crowded elevator down to the parking garage he whispered under his breath, "I hope she never tells that girl the true meaning of that name."

Angela and "L" were released from the hospital after a three day stay and the Matthews family had begun. Life looked good on Park Avenue for Gregory and Angela. That's what their friends and family thought, but looks can be quite deceiving. The Matthews lived in a penthouse apartment that overlooked Central Park. Their servants consisted of a maid, a butler, and Glen, the chauffeur. Gregory had built up a lucrative stock brokerage business in relatively short order. Many of his clients were the wealthy and powerful of New York. He owed all that to his father-in-law.

Angela developed into a housewife that loved her soap operas, but cared for little else. She dove into the bottle while Gregory dove into work. Liquor stole Angela's beauty, and sleeping in the same bed with her husband became a thing of the past. Gregory began to work from daylight to dark and their marriage became even more fragmented than it already was. The one bright spot for Gregory was "L". Of course, "L" got the best schooling that money could buy. Only the best private schools would do. Pre-school soon passed, then elementary school, and in just a few short years "L" had become a teenager.

It was another cool New York evening when Gregory finally got home. He looked in on "L" as he did from time to time and much to his surprise she was still awake.

"Happy birthday sweetheart.   You're 18 now, right?"

"Funny, Dad." She giggled. "14."

"What'd you get for your birthday?"

"Mom had Glen go get some Barbies. They weren't even wrapped and they still had the price tags on them. I didn't even get a cake or card!"

"Well, I guess you don't want this then?"

Gregory pulled out a stuffed Teddy Bear from his overcoat.

"Oh, Dad!"

"L" hugged the bear, then her dad.

"Read the card that's taped to his feet."

She read out loud, "I'm sorry for the way things are. I want you to remember something, I love you and always will! Dad."

"L" started crying.

"Dad, what are we going to do about Mom?"

"Sweetheart, Mom's angry at the world and she
doesn't want anybody's help.   There's not much
anyone can do when a person is in that kind of
shape."

"Dad, do you regret marrying Mom?"

"Why would you ask something like that?"

"Because she's been saying that about you
lately."

"Your Mom gave me you. I don't regret that."

"Let's not talk about that anymore, OK?"

"OK."

"Night, sweetheart."

"Goodnight, Dad."

Gregory walked into the kitchen and noticed
there were several broken items on the counter and
floor. He recognized many of them to be wedding
gifts. Angela walked into the room with a drink in
her hand and Gregory could tell she was quite
drunk.

"You're a wreck. Get yourself together or enroll
in the Betty Ford clinic."

"Screw you!"

"That booze is going to kill you someday!"

"Greg, I've been thinking."

"Oh Yeah, about what?"

"A divorce."

"Your dad wouldn't like that too much, now
would he?"

"My life's hell now, what difference does it
make?"

"Oh, go sleep it off!"

Angela never said another word as she retreated
to her room where she passed out on the bed.

The next day dawned and Gregory went to work. He received a phone call from "L" around three in the afternoon.

"Dad, you're got to come home!"

"Why, sweetheart? What's wrong?"

"Mom's throwing all your clothes and stuff in the hallway. She keeps yelling, 'It's over!'"

Gregory made his way home to find a note pinned to the front door. It read, "I'm throwing you out of my life!" Gregory's belongings were scattered throughout the hall. As he stood there looking at what Angela had done, one particular item caught his eye. It was his backpack from his college days at ORU. It looked the same as it did fifteen years earlier. In his mind he thought, "That's the only thing her dad didn't pay for." Gregory bent over to pick up the backpack and walked out of the building and Angela's life forever.

Gregory walked for what seemed like hours. His mind became consumed with the thoughts of his dad and how he had become just like him. Before long it was dark.

He had strolled into Times Square when he heard singing. It was coming from a church there. The thought raced through his mind, "Go in!" Immediately another thought raced through his mind. "You can't. You turned your back on God!"

As he looked down he noticed a tract laying on the sidewalk. He bent down to pick it up. The printed verse on that torn page jumped out at him. It was Isaiah 41:10, his favorite. Gregory decided to walk into the service. He kept quoting that verse. "Fear not, I am with you. I will help you."

The praise and worship portion of the service was going on and it brought back memories of his college days, but this service wasn't anything like he had experienced before. There were black people there, white people, a few Orientals and even an Indian or two. That wasn't something he was used to, but he was beginning to like it. Gregory stood against the wall in the back of the church until things got quiet. He knew from his experiences at ORU what was coming next, the altar call. As he made his way to the door to exit someone blocked his path. It was a young punker. His hair stood straight up with spikes of many colors.

"Mister, I don't know what you're going through, but something told me to stop you before you walked out that door. I just feel like tellin' ya Jesus loves you!"

Tears started to roll down Gregory's face. The young man grabbed Gregory and hugged him.

He whispered in his ear, "I'm Chuck, I love you man! Will you go to the altar with me? Will ya let Jesus rule?"

Gregory's tears became a steady flow and he nodded his head. Both men walked to the front, bowed down, and repeated the sinner's prayer. Gregory had finally accepted Jesus for real this time.

The service had ended long before and Gregory was still lying on the floor praying. The pastor approached him and said, "Lock the door when you leave, son." Gregory nodded.

Gregory had never experienced anything like that, he was quite literally a new man. During his prayers he would ask, "Lord, what do I do?" This thought repeatedly passed through his consciousness. "Take your backpack and experience my creation, my son. Cleanse your soul and those of others."

Was it a message from God? Gregory certainly thought so. He left the church with a new agenda. He walked to an ATM machine and withdrew a few hundred dollars. He then called his old roommate, James.

"Hello!"

"James?"

"Yeah, who is it?"

"It's Greg."

"Do you know what time it is?"

"I need a favor."

"What is it?'

"Angela threw me out. She's filing for divorce. James, I got saved tonight! I'm quitting my job and I'm leaving to journey across the country to cleanse my soul."

"What? Are you drunk?"

"Nope, stone sober!"

"You're not serious, right?"

"I couldn't be more serious."

"What is it you want me to do?"

"Invest the money and put the interest in that account of ours. That one we started a long time ago. You know, the one Angela never found out about?"

"OK, but how will you live?"

"With the Lord's help … one day at a time!"

"You know what this means, don't you?"

"What?"

"You'll never work on Wall Street again!"

"That's obvious."

"OK, I'll keep money in that account so you can use the ATM if you need it."

"Thanks."

"Are you sure this is something you want to do? It sure does sound far out."

"It's something I have to do!"

"Ok … good luck. If you need anything, just call me."

"Got it!"

"Bye, Greg."

"Bye, James."

At the exact moment Gregory hung up the phone Becky Stover was being awakened by a dream in Oklahoma. She dreamed of Gregory that night and it troubled her. She woke up and immediately knelt beside her bed. She felt a tremendous power come over her. It was stronger than she had ever felt before. The thought rushed through her mind, "Pray!" Becky cried while praying, so loud that it woke her parents up.

When her parents walked into the room they said, "Becky, what's wrong?"

"Mom, Dad, it's Greg. Something's wrong!"

Becky's mother and father were no strangers to prayer. They knelt down beside her and prayed with her until dawn. You see, they still loved Gregory with all their heart, as did Becky.

Born To Serve

The hour was late when Gregory ended his telephone conversation. He was quite tired and began to walk down 7th Ave. He thought to himself, a five-star hotel would be nice about right now, but destiny had a different set of plans drawn that evening. As he walked down the street he became preoccupied with the names on the store fronts across the street. Gregory walked a few blocks when he noticed an establishment that really caught his eye. The name on that particular storefront said, *The Rock on 7th Ave.*

Gregory became quite curious and decided to walk across the street to check the place out. As he drew closer he realized it was a mission, a homeless shelter. He had never visited a place like that before. A small voice began to speak to his conscious, it said, "Stay here!" He noticed that the lights were off. He pressed his face to the glass and peered through the window. "There's people in there," he thought.

They were on cots and appeared to be asleep. Gregory quietly reached for the door handle and turned it. Much to his surprise, the door was unlocked. He walked in and followed the dimly lit hallway that led to the room where the homeless were sleeping. Gregory noticed there were a couple of empty cots in the corner and decided to spend the

night on one of them when he accidentally bumped one of the occupied ones. He thought the noise would wake those sleeping, but it didn't. As he knelt down to apologize for the incident he noticed that the man looked familiar. With the man still asleep, Gregory got within a few inches of his face and began to stare. He thought to himself, "I know this guy! Where do I know him from? Think, Greg, think! I got it, I remember now." Gregory started crying. He laid his hands on the man's arm and began to pray silently. Gregory wasn't aware of it, but he was being watched. After he finished praying, he
stood. A voice then emerged from the shadows. "May I help you?"
 "Sorry."
 "Your new here, aren't you?"
 "Yes."
 "Want a cup of coffee?"
 "Please."
Gregory followed the stranger to the back of the building where the kitchen was.
 "Have a seat, I'll turn the lights on and make a pot."
 "Thanks."
 "By the way, how do you like it?"
 "Pardon me?"
 "Your coffee, how do you like it?"
 "Oh, black."
After a few minutes the stranger handed Gregory a cup and said, "There you go."
 "Thanks."
 "Mind if I have a seat with you?

"No, go right ahead."

The stranger extended his hand from across the table and introduced himself. "Hi, I'm Peter, I run this place."

"Gregory Matthews."

"Nice to meet ya. Tell me, what was going on in there?"

"I prayed for a homeless guy, that's all."

"I know that, but why him? Why him out of all those guys?"

"It's a long story."

"Man, I got all night!"

"You first."

"What?"

"You go first. What's your story? To be honest, you look more like a biker than you do a businessman."

"Ok then. Well, first of all, I was a biker once, but Jesus changed all that. Now I'm a businessman. I'm in the business of saving souls.

"What changed you?"

"I wrecked my bike in Times Square one night. I accidentally ran into a wall of a church."

"For real? A church?"

"Yeah … a church. Well, I figured they'd call the police, but they didn't. Believe it or not, some bikers that I knew came outside when they heard the noise. I asked 'em what they were doin' there! They told me they were going to that church. I said, 'No way!' Well, to make a long story short, I walked in and have never been the same again. Now, it's your turn. Tell me, how do you know Jim?"

"Who?"

"Jim Smith. The guy you prayed for a little bit ago. You acted like you knew him."

"I recognized him from Wall Street."

"From his days at Q-tech?"

"Q-tech? What's Q-tech?"

"I thought you said you knew him?"

"I'm ashamed to admit this."

"Admit what?"

"When I looked at him in there, I recognized him from my days of being a broker on Wall Street. He used to sit in a cardboard box outside the Stock Exchange. When he asked me for money I always refused. A lot of times something told me to take him home, but I always ignored it … I was a jerk back then!"

"I think I understand now. So, you really didn't know about Jim and his company, did you?"

"Know what?"

"Jim owned a company called Q-tech. Started it out of his garage in '67. He was into high-tech research. It even went fortune 500."

"What in the world happened?"

"Well, Jim was the victim of a hostile take-over. The board sold the controlling shares to another company and fired him. When the money ran out his wife left him. He lost everything, that's when he dove into the bottle. When he tells people that story they don't believe him."

"Why?"

"Think about it, who's going to believe a homeless drunk. The sad part of it is … it's true."

"I can relate to that."

"You can? So, what brings you our way?"

"I'm on a journey."

"Journey? What kind of journey?"

"A soul cleansing one. I feel like I'm supposed to walk to L.A."

"Now, that would be God!"

"You don't think I'm nuts?"

"No, why should I?"

"I figured you would."

"Gregory, experience says when God speaks, we listen. If we want His blessing, we obey."

"Thanks, Pete. Can I call you Pete?"

"Sure. Hey, we better get some shut-eye."

Peter retired to his room and Gregory to his cot and both soon drifted off to sleep.

Morning came and the residents were fed breakfast. As Gregory moved through the serving line he noticed that Peter was standing behind the counter.

"Good morning, Gregory. Sleep well?"

"Yes, yes I did. Hey, where's Jim? I don't see him."

"He always leaves before breakfast."

"That's too bad. I wish I could have spoken to him."

"Before he left this morning, he told me he knew you were praying for him last night. He said he acted like he was asleep. He said he remembered who you were. His quote was, "A great Wall Street mind.""

"He did?"

"Yeah. By the way, what prayer did you pray over him last night?"

"I prayed for restoration."

"Good!"

After Gregory finished his breakfast it came time to leave and say goodbye to his new found friend. He stretched forth his hand and simply said, "Thanks, Peter."

"Before you leave Gregory, can I pray for ya?"

"I would like that."

"Father, plan, guide, and protect my brother on this trip. May he convey your love to everyone he meets. Lord, I thank you for allowing our paths to cross. Go forth and be blessed. In Jesus's holy name, we pray, Amen."

"Amen. Thanks, Pete."

"Bye, my friend."

"Bye."

Gregory's opinion of the homeless was never the same after that. Gregory walked out the mission's doors that day and into the open arms of the world.

His journey began with a stroll down New York's 7th Ave, and within a matter of minutes the Holland Tunnel came into sight. Gregory approached the entrance to the tunnel and walked right past the toll booth. The attendant inside yelled, "Hey!" Gregory never heard him and kept walking. The attendant stepped out the back door of the booth and yelled.

"Hey! Hey you! Stop!"

Gregory turned around to look at the attendant without saying a word.

"Get your butt over here!"

"What's the problem officer?"

"First of all, I'm not a cop. And what in the world do you think you're doin'?"

"Walking to New Jersey!"

"No, you're not!"

"I was always told its free to exit New York through the tunnel."

"It is, but we're on alert. No foot traffic!" After a moment of silence the attendant said, "Humm, if you make it worth my while I'll look the other way."

"You mean a bribe, right?"

"Bribe is such an ugly word.   Pay-up, or take a hike, pal!"

"How much will this over-site cost me?"

By that time, the vehicle traffic at the toll booth was backing up. Drivers were beginning to roll down their windows and yell obscenities.

"What's it goin' be, pal!"

"How much?"

"A hundred bucks!"

Gregory reached in his pocket and handed the man a one hundred dollar bill.

"See ya … sucker!"

Gregory hung his head and walked away. The attendant stepped back into the toll booth, laughing.

After the vehicle traffic filed through and Gregory had walked a few hundred yards a car pulled over along side the platform where he was walking. The elderly female driver rolled down her window.

"Young man! Would you please come here?"

Gregory thought to himself, "What now?"

"Yes, Maam?"

"As I was watching your conversation with that man from my car, something told me to give you a hundred dollars. I've lived long enough to know His voice. Here!"

The elderly lady handed Gregory a brand new one hundred dollar bill and drove off.

Gregory turned around and walked away. As he did, he looked down at the hand that held the bill, and said, "Cool!"

It took Gregory almost an hour to reach the other side of the Hudson, but when he did, he thought, "Next stop, Hoboken!"

As Gregory toured the streets of Hoboken he noticed a dollar store. He thought to himself, "I need some supplies for that backpack." Once inside, Gregory began to fill his cart with necessities. Gregory grabbed a package of pens and paper from the shelf and opened them. The clerk yelled, "You're gonna pay for that!"

Gregory said, "I will!"

Gregory made a list of supplies he needed. It read as follows:

1) Toothpaste and brush
2) Comb
3) Shoes, socks
4) Shirt
5) Blue jeans
6) Map
7) Food
8) Jacket
9) Matches
10) Sleeping bag
11) Journal

12) Bible

As Gregory wheeled his cart to the check-out he could tell the young teenage girl behind the counter wasn't very happy with him. She stood and stared while chomping her gum. Gregory removed the items from the cart and placed them on the counter. After she finished ringing it up, she said, "That'll be $210.80."

Gregory said, "What's that?" as he pointed his finger at something behind her.

"What's what?"

"That hat hanging up there?"

"I don't know!"

"Can I see it?"

The clerk grabbed the hat hanging on the wall and threw it on the counter.

"There! You're holding up the line!"

"Am I missing something?"

"What?"

"I'm the only one in line!"

"Just hurry up, I ain't got all day!"

As Gregory stood there staring at the hat, he made the comment, "Where did you get this?"

"I don't know, come on, bubby!"

"Young lady, what is your problem?"

"You!"

As Gregory looked at her name tag, he said, "Lisa, I'm not the problem, but your unhappiness with life is."

"Thanks preacher!"

"Why'd you call me that?"

"You bought a Bible, didn't ya?"

"Yeah."

"Are you going to buy the hat, or not?"

Gregory began to stare at the hat once again. The hat had a logo embroidered on it. The logo consisted of a construction worker holding a Bible with the words *Builder of the Spirit* spelled out in tools.

"I like that! That's what I wanna be!"

"Be what?"

"A Builder of the Spirit."

"What ever! If ya want the hat it'll be another $16.50."

"I'll take it!"

"Great! Pay me $227.30!"

Gregory handed her $250.00 and started to walk out the door.

The clerk yelled, "Hey, you paid me too much!"

Gregory answered by saying, "Keep the change, Lisa," and he walked out the door. He then walked across the street to the donut shop to grab a cup of coffee. Shortly after he took a seat, Lisa walked in.

Lisa walked over to Gregory's table and threw his change on it.

"I seen you come in here! I followed you over here, just to tell ya, I don't need a hand-out! There's your money!"

"Lisa, have a seat."

"I don't think so! I just clocked out and I wanna go home."

"Please!"

"Ok, but I want you to know that I know everybody in here. They're watchin', so don't get any stupid ideas!"

"Waitress! A couple of coffees … please."

"I don't drink coffee!"

"A coffee and a coke then."

Gregory and Lisa conversed for quite some time. Her anger seemed to melt away with the passage of time. Over the course of the next two hours, Lisa proceeded to tell her life story. It was one of divorce, abuse and rape.

"Greg, I haven't been able to trust anyone for a long time, but you seem different than all the rest."

"I'm nothing, but I know the most trustworthy guy on the planet."

"Who's that?"

"Jesus."

"Here we go again!"

"No, listen to me. Everybody else has failed you, right?"

"Right!"

"Why not give Him a try!"

"How can you trust someone you can't even see?"

"You trust Him in your heart, Lisa. That's where He lives."

"He wouldn't want to live in mine, it's cold. It's been that way for a long time." Lisa began to cry.

"Would you like for Him to come into your heart?"

"I'm beyond help, preacher."

"Lisa, God loves you so much that He sent his only son to die for you. Jesus died so you might live."

"He died for me?" Lisa was crying even harder by now.

"If you're tired of the old life, give Him a chance."

"If it's that easy, tell me what to do."

"Close your eyes and repeat these words after me, Jesus."

"Jesus."

"I've made a mess out of my life."

"I've made a mess out of my life."

"I believe you died on the cross for my sins and you rose from the dead on the third day."

"I believe you died on the cross for my sins and you rose from the dead on the third day.

"You truly are the son of God!"

"You truly are the son of God!"

"Forgive me of my sin and wash me pure, like snow."

"Forgive me of my sin and wash me pure, like snow."

"Thank you, Lord, for saving me!"

"Thank you, Lord, for saving me!"

"Lisa, that was the most important decision you will ever make in your life. You will never be the same again."

"I feel better already, preacher."

Gregory stood up to shake her hand and say goodbye.

"I got to go. You're goin' to be fine, kiddo."

Lisa stood to say, "You know somethin'? I haven't given anybody a hug in a long time. Would you mind one?"

"That's the best offer I've had all day."

Lisa wrapped her arms around Gregory and gave him a tender hug and a kiss on the cheek. She whispered in his ear, "Thanks preacher."

Horizon

As Gregory was leaving the city limits of Hoboken, he noticed the town sign. He laughed and mumbled, "Holy Graffiti!" Gregory read out loud, *Thank you for visiting Hoboken,* and *Jesus is Lord* that was spray painted on the bottom of the sign. Gregory then fell to his knees in front of the sign and placed his hand on it.

"Lord, if what happened back there with Lisa is your plan, I can't wait for this journey to begin. Give me wisdom and strength for what lies ahead. Drench me with your Spirit, that I can make a difference. Amen."

The day was still early and Gregory would eventually make his way to the Jersey City limits. From there, it was onto 12th Street and Interstate 78.

As Gregory stood, staring at the Interstate, he experienced a presence come over him like never before. He had heard other students at ORU speak of the Holy Spirit and their experiences, but he was never privileged to it. At that moment, his newly purchased Bible fell to the ground from his backpack. It fell open to Isaiah 5:16. The words, "The Holy God will show himself," continually rang in his head.

Gregory mumbled to himself, "I understand, Lord." He repeatedly nodded his head, as to say, "I understand now." The spiritual entity remained, it felt much like static electricity, but in a good way. Thoughts began to flood his mind. Thoughts like, "Walk, don't ride the journey." "Man created that which lies before you." "Travel it, but seek first my hand and will first."

Gregory thought to himself, "That's it! That's how you speak to your people! You place your thought in their minds."

Gregory yelled to the sky, "Oh, thank you, Lord, thank you!"

Gregory came away from the experience with the feeling he was to walk everywhere he went. He was to follow the Interstate system, but not totally rely on it. The surrounding communities are where the miracles are going to be!

It was starting to get late in the day when he crossed the Newark bay into Newark. He thought to himself, "I really don't want to sleep in the city, I'd like to sleep under the stars." Shortly before dust he exited the Newark city limits. As it grew dark, Gregory thought, "I wish I knew what time it was?" He had forgotten to purchase a watch. He mumbled to himself. "It doesn't matter anyway, it's not like I'm in a hurry or something."

Gregory decided to venture away from 78. He thought to himself, "If I'm to meet people, I can't stay on that gray monster all the time."

He realized it was quite late and the heaviness of the day was taking its toll on him. He came across a bullet ridden sign, that said, *Welcome to Basking Ridge*.

Talking to himself, as he often did, Gregory said, "This looks like as good a place as any." Gregory unfolded his sleeping bag and swept in the field right under the sign. He was so tired he didn't even bother making a fire, he drifted off to sleep almost immediately.

Morning came, and Gregory began to smell the aroma of biscuits.   He thought to himself, "I love biscuits and gravy!"

He leaned against a neighboring oak and said, "Bless this town, Lord, and its people!"

As Gregory strolled down King George Road, he began to realize where the smell was coming from. It was coming from the Baptist church on the hill. As he walked past the church several children inside yelled.

"Hey, look at the man with the backpack!"

Pastor Tim peered out the window to see what all the excitement was about. He said, "Hey, kids! Would you like to invite a stranger to breakfast?"

Two little girls grabbed each of the pastor's hands and began to pull him towards the door. They ran down the steps and over the hill to the road below. Pastor Tim and the girls approached Gregory from behind.

The Pastor said, "Break bread with us, brother."

Gregory turned around to say, "Are you talking to me?"

One of the little girls giggled.

Gregory bent down to say, "What's so funny?"

"You ... silly! We're the only ones out here."

"You got a point."

The Pastor held out his hand to say, "I'm Tim. I shepherd the flock on the hill that's staring out the window at us."

"I'm Greg, glad to meet you pastor. I would be honored to eat with you."

One of the little girls pulled on Pastor Tim's pant leg. When he bent down, she whispered in his ear, "We did a good thing, didn't we?"

He nodded his head.

As Gregory, the pastor, and the girls approached the front steps he noticed people were filing out the front door to hug him. Obviously, he wasn't used to all that attention. Men, women, and children alike, began to hug him.

"Greg, let's go inside. Do you like biscuits and gravy?"

Gregory nodded his head and smiled.

Tim and his wife sat across the table from Gregory.

"So, tell me, what brings you to these parts?"

Gregory was quite hungry. As he stuffed his mouth he said, "God's got me on a journey."

"I believe He does! I knew from the moment I saw you there was something about ya, call it a feeling, I guess."

"By the way, Pastor. Why is everybody here on a Saturday morning?"

Pastor Tim informed Gregory that today was habitat day. Gregory had no idea what that was.

"We have been helping a low income family build a home there in town."

"I see!" Gregory had a worried look on his face.

"It's not what you think. I didn't drag you in here to get free labor."

"The thought may have crossed my mind. But since you put it that way."

Gregory went back to stuffing his face.

Pastor Tim looked troubled. After a few moments of silence he said, "And?"

Gregory looked at him, removed the napkin from his lap, placed it on the table in front of him and pushed himself away from the table.

"I guess I better get going."

"You're leaving?"

"Yeah."

"Well, good luck."

Gregory didn't get more than a few hundred yards down the hill and onto the road until something told him to go back.   Gregory turned around and walked back to the church and through the front door.

"Forget something, Greg?"

"Yeah, my manners! I may not know much about construction, but God's working on this one. I'm sorry Pastor, sorry for being a jerk."

One of the little girls, who greeted Gregory, ran up to him and hugged his leg.

"I love jerks!" The little one said.

Laughs rang out.

The entire church congregation worked on the house that day. Gregory learned from the workers that the couple had lost everything in a fire and they didn't have insurance. The church was paying for the construction of the home. Someone estimated the cost to be around $50,000.00.

At the end of the day, Pastor Tim tried to convince Gregory to spend the night at his place, but he would have no part of it. Gregory persuaded the couple to allow him a night on the floor of their new home. They couldn't understand why he wanted to do such a thing, but they consented to his wishes.

Gregory walked to the town's pool hall that night and phoned James. He told him to wait a couple of days and then wire $50,000.00 to Pastor Tim. He also instructed James to send a note with it. The note was to simply say, "Proverbs 24:3."

Gregory did indeed sleep on the floor of that new home that night. Before he fell asleep he walked around the house with his Bible in hand and blessed every door and window with a short prayer.

Gregory awoke early the next day to get back on the road, all without saying goodbye. As he left the city limits, he said, "Lord, bless Basking Ridge!"

The next few days took Gregory on a venture through the New Jersey countryside. He wondered upon an old truck stop along State Road 206. The sign ahead said, Pottersville 8 miles, but *The Garden Truck Stop* looked too inviting to pass by. The place looked run down but the thought of a cheeseburger and fries just sounded too tempting. Gregory walked in and sat down at a booth. It was hard for him to make out, but it sounded like preaching coming from the other room. After he ordered his food he decided to take his plate into the other room and eat his meal in there. No sooner than he sat down he was welcomed by an elderly lady.

"Hi stranger, I'm Mabelle. I'm the owner of this place. Welcome to the truckers Tuesday night Bible study. Tell these good olde boys your name."

As Gregory waved to everybody in the room, he said, "Hi, I'm Greg.

Some of the guys in the room said hello, but most just nodded their heads. Gregory listened for over an hour to Mabelle. He thought to himself, "She's good!"

After the study was over, Mabelle sat down at the booth where Gregory was.

"So, what's your story, stranger?"

"I'm on a journey, Mabelle."

"I see that! I hope it's for the right reasons."

"I assure you … it is."

"Get enough to eat?"

"Yes, and it tasted great."

"Glad to serve!"

"Tell me about this place, would you?"

"Well, my husband, God rest his soul."

"Oh, I'm sorry!"

"No, don't be. He's in a better place than we are."

Gregory nodded his head several times.

"Well, like I was saying, he was a long haul trucker for years. When he retired we bought this place. About five years back he got cancer."

A tear welled up in Mabelle's eye, as did Gregory's.

"A friend of his led both of us to Christ shortly before he died. Before my husband died he made me promise to tell the truckers that God loves em'.

His friend helped me with this place before he died.
It was his idea to have the Bible study in there."

"I'm sorry to hear that, when did he die?"

"Last month."

Mabelle and Gregory talked for what seemed
like hours, but it was time for him to hit the road
again.

"Can I pray for ya before you go?" Mabelle
asked.

"I'd like that."

She wrapped her old rough, but tender hands
around his. "Father, you see his heart! Help him!
In your Son's holy name. Amen."

Mabelle walked to the counter and placed a
couple of burgers in a sack. "That's for the road."

"Thanks, Mabelle."

Gregory left and walked a mile or so down the
road. He turned around and said, "Lord, bless that
place!"

Gregory made his way back towards Interstate
78. A couple of days later he found himself
walking through the town of Lebanon on Route 22.
His curiosity was aroused when he heard laughing
and singing coming from the *His Way Diner* as he
passed by. After he walked in he removed his
backpack and sat down at the counter. He didn't
notice that he was the only white person in there
until after the diner became silent. He finally
noticed he was out of place when he spun around on
his stool. While all eyes were on him he felt a tap
on his shoulder. A voice from behind him said,
"What'll it be … Boy?"

"A song and a prayer?" Gregory jokingly said, "But if you don't mind, the special."

"Not funny … Boy!"

A voice from behind the grill said, "Oh, leave him alone, Henry!"

"Quiet … Woman!" The black waiter said.

The heavy set black woman removed her apron and marched out to the counter. Getting up in Henry's face, she said, "Henry Bowles, you may think you own this place, but I run it!   If you still want this wife, you better shut your mouth! Now apologize to that man!"

All eyes were fixed on the couple's argument by now. Henry hung his head and raised his hand to Gregory. They shook hands. After that, everything went back to normal. Three girls were sitting in the booth behind Gregory and he heard them singing quietly among themselves. Gregory spun around on his stool, looked at the girls, and said, "I'd like to hear more."

One of the girls said, "We're shy around strangers. Besides, our Mamas say we can't sing anything but gospel."

Gregory said, "That's fine."

After the girls talked among themselves for a minute they started singing *Amazing Grace*. Before long, almost everyone in the diner was singing, including Gregory. He would eventually leave there, but he did so with a sense of peace and assurance.

Several more nights of sleeping under the stars passed before the Pennsylvania border came into sight.   As he watched the border from his campfire that night, he thought, "That town, Alpha, is the only thing standing in my way!" Gregory finally went to sleep, but he didn't sleep very well. All night long he thought he heard angels singing. It left him with an uneasy feeling the next day.

Gregory put out the campfire that morning and walked to town. As he walked through the outskirts of Alpha he noticed a large tent. It reminded him of the pictures he saw on the walls at ORU. He knew that Oral Roberts, the founder of ORU, preached in tents like that back in the 50's.

As he drew closer, he saw several people carrying signs. It appeared that they were protesting something. They were marching in a circle, shouting, "False prophet." Their signs said, "Don't be deceived, Evangelist T. James Bradley is a false prophet. Read Matthew 7:15 and 24:11." Gregory didn't get far past the protestors when he heard sirens. As he stood from afar, he watched the arrival of the police. He could hear the officer tell the protestors to stop but they didn't listen. The officer told them they were breaking the law because they didn't have a permit, "Unlawful assembly", he called it. The protestors kept marching and shouting, the more the officer talked, the louder they got. He finally said, "That's it, you're going to jail." Gregory could hear him calling for back-up on the radio. Several squad cars soon arrived and all the protestors were handcuffed and taken into custody.

The last squad car left, and Gregory stood there wondering why those people would go to such extremes. He continued his walk to town, and as he passed the library he decided to research this man that everybody was so upset about. Gregory found many articles there about T. James Bradley. Most of them called him a "Controversial faith healer." Gregory thought, "I'll just see for myself."

Gregory entered the tent that night, but not before withdrawing some money from an ATM machine. Gregory stood at the rear of the tent so he wouldn't be noticed. After a few songs the preacher began his sermon. He hadn't spoke long when he pointed to the rear of the tent.

"You … young man!"

Gregory pointed to his chest, as to say, "Me?"

"Yes … you! Come forward."

Gregory removed his backpack and walked to the front. As he stood there, with the preacher, he thought, "I'm standing here, with T. James Bradley!"

T. James had Gregory turn to face the audience. When he did that, the preacher placed his arm over his shoulder.

Speaking into the microphone, T. James said, "You're on a journey, ordained by God, aren't you?" Then he put the microphone to Gregory's mouth.

"Yes, but how did you know that?"

T. James Bradley placed a finger over his own mouth, as to say, "Be quiet." Then he whispered in Gregory's ear, "The Spirit said, 'You are to give $50.00 of that five hundred you withdrew from the bank.'"

Gregory thought to himself, "How's he know that?"

Speaking into the microphone again, T. James Bradley said, "Your name is Gregory, and God's calling you to be His watchman. You will find what you seek in Los Angeles. You will preach the gospel to the poor, the poor in spirit, and be a builder for the kingdom. Gregory, the Spirit keeps saying, 'Isaiah 41:10.'"

After the preacher finished speaking, he had Gregory return to his seat. Gregory sat down in amazement. He thought to himself, "There's no way that man could know all that, he's not a false prophet!"

When the offering plate came around Gregory threw a one hundred dollar bill in it. It was late in the evening when the service ended and Gregory decided to head back to his previous campsite. Before falling asleep that night Gregory wrote in his journal, "Two nights in a row I have heard angels singing. I keep hearing in my head, 'I am the beginning, follow to the end.'"

The Vision

The morning sun streamed through the rustling leaves of the trees to wake our traveler, it was a new day! Gregory stirred the coals of the campfire in preparation for breakfast. The eggs were cooking and Gregory began a journal entry.

"March 21."

"A little over a hundred miles from New York and a couple of weeks into the trip. I'm beginning to see God's plan for my life unfold.   I'm crossing over into Pennsylvania today. Lord, thanks for the New Jersey experience!"

Gregory closed the journal and laid back against a rock to enjoy his eggs. He finished breakfast, extinguished the fire, and packed up.   Interstate 78 was waiting and so was the Pennsylvania border.

The Interstate is a busy yet lonely place, as the day would unveil.   With a stiff breeze in his face, and a stick to chew on, Gregory never ventured far from 78 that day. Although few and far between, some cars would pull over to give him a ride, but he always refused. He crossed the border during the early morning hours and by late afternoon he noticed the little town of Bethlehem.

"I wonder if they have room at the Inn? The Holiday Inn!"

As soon as Gregory spoke those words a tree limb fell in his path.

Gregory looked to the sky and said, "Sorry Lord! It was just a joke."

He followed the main road that led to town. A billboard soon caught his eye. It read, "Welcome to the Christmas City. Home of Bethlehem Steel. Population 75,000." Across the vast field was the steel plant, with multiple colored smoke coming from its stacks. Gregory made camp that evening in a nearby woods.

Some days later, he would record journal entries about stops made in Stony Run, Bethel, Ono, and Middle Sex. After following Interstate 81 for a short time he then found himself on the concrete trail called I-76.

Newville soon came over the horizon. A small sign advertising a KOA campground two miles to the left, caught Gregory's attention. That looked like an excellent invitation to the tired traveler.

An older couple owned the campground and they were very kind and considerate to their new visitor.

"Hi, we're the Smiths. I'm Jim, and this is my wife Dorothy. Have ya ever camped with us before?"

"No, I haven't."

"Modern or primitive?"

"Excuse me?"

"Do you need hook-up for your RV?"

Gregory jokingly told the couple his RV was on his back.

"I see, roughing it! Dorothy, give this young man our best primitive spot."

Dorothy told Gregory it was site three, just over the hill by the water falls.

Evening was soon to come and Gregory unrolled his sleeping bag on the ground. After he returned from the shower house he found a note lying on his sleeping bag. It read, "If you don't want to spend the night alone come to site one." Gregory didn't know what to make of the note, but his curiosity got the best of him. He found a young couple stirring the fire at site one.

"Excuse me, I got this note."

"We wrote that," they answered together.

Gregory noticed a Bible laying on the picnic table beside their tent.

"I see you have a Bible. Are you guys Christians?"

"Yes, we are. I'm sorry, I'm David Linton and this is my wife Lynn. We were going to camp with a couple we're friends with, but they had to cancel at the last minute. You looked lonely over there and we have a spare tent if you want some company tonight."

Gregory accepted their offer. He moved his stuff over to their site and both men pitched the spare tent while Lynn cooked supper.

"Thanks for inviting me over." Gregory said to David.

"No problem."

"So, where are you guys from?"

"Harrisburg."

"What do ya do there?" Gregory asked.

"We are the youth pastors at the Harrisburg Christian Church. And you?"

"I'm on my way to L.A."

"Why? That's a long way!"

"It's a God thing!"

David laughed. "We can relate to that, can't we Lynn?"

"Yes … we can."

All three talked until the hour became late. Before retiring for the night the couple prayed for Gregory. He appreciated their thoughtful prayer.

Gregory took to the road once again early that morning, he didn't have the heart to wake his new found friends to say goodbye.

A couple of nights later he camped beside a bridge near Crystal Spring and three days after that he found himself wandering down 31 near Brotherton.

Gregory heard what he thought was a vehicle approaching. As he crested the hill he saw a tractor coming. It was a farmer hauling a large bale of hay on an older model John Deere. The farmer stopped in front of Gregory and waited for him to approach. Gregory walked a few paces past the tractor and the farmer shut it off. He yelled, "Hi!" Gregory turned and walked towards the man who already had his hand extended.

They shook hands and the farmer said, "I don't have to ask ya what brings ya our way. I can tell you're either running to something or away from it."

"Something like that." Gregory replied.

"The farmhouse is just down the road. Hop on board, you look like you could use a hot meal."

"Are you sure?"

"I'm sure."

Gregory extended his hand once again and said, "I'm Gregory Matthews. And your name is?"

"John will do."

John fired the *Old girl* up and they traveled at a snails pace back to the house. They parked the tractor and made their way to the front door. John and Gregory removed their shoes once inside and John yelled, "Honey, we got company!"

"Have a seat, Gregory," John said.

Gregory sat down at the couple's dining room table. "This sure is nice of you. You guys sure are trusting."

"I wouldn't have invited you in if He hadn't told me to."

"Who's he?"

John stood and stared out the dining room window to say nothing.

"Who's he?" Gregory repeated.

John stood there and stared at his farm through the window. He lowered his head and placed his hand over his face and began to weep. "I'm beginning to think that even He can't save us now."

"Who's he?" Gregory asked.

John's wife saw his tears and walked over to where her husband was standing. She gave him a hug.

"Sweetheart, God can do anything!"

Both John and his wife stood hugging, while the tears streamed down their faces.

Gregory knew that something was wrong. The thought raced through his mind, "I have you here for a reason." Now he understood the "He" they were talking about.

Gregory thought he would break the ice by saying, "Would it be inconvenient to ask what's for supper?"

Julie giggled and wiped the tears from her face. She walked back to the kitchen. She emerged with a large plate of fried chicken.

"That's the main course, guys. I got mashed potatoes and gravy too. I may even have a slice of apple pie or two out there."

All three sat down to eat and John insisted on praying over the meal.

"Father, I believe your word. It says you will never leave us or forsake us, I believe that. I thank you for what food we have, and give me strength for what's coming. Amen."

Gregory raised his head to say, "What's coming?"

"Nothing." John replied.

"I know better than that. Something's bad wrong here."

John looked across the table at Gregory and said, "Just enjoy your meal and you can be on your way."

"I'm not going anywhere until you tell me what's going on!"

Julie said, "It's personal."

We all know He brought me here to help. "How can I help if I don't know what the problem is?"

John laughed, "This place is doomed."

"Doomed?"

"That's right, doomed! The bank's calling in the note next week."

"Why?"

"We got behind on the payments because the herd hasn't been producing much milk lately. The bank doesn't seem too willing to work with us either."

The thought "Sleep in the barn" occurred to Gregory.

"John, can I sleep in your barn tonight? You know, before I hit the trail tomorrow?"

"You don't have to sleep out there, we got a spare bedroom."

"You don't understand. He told me to."

"Who's He?"

Gregory said, "You know."

John nodded his head repeatedly to say, "Yeah."

Gregory walked out the door and towards the barn. John held the door open and yelled, " I'll see you in the morning, I milk at five."

Gregory waved his hand in the air to say OK.

Darkness fell upon the farm and Gregory eventually drifted off to sleep. An angel appeared to him in a dream that night. The setting of the dream appeared to be heaven and he was sitting on a rock. The angel told Gregory his name was Gabriel and that Gregory was the angel's assignment. The angel told of a great work ahead and many miracles to follow.

Gregory woke to a startled feeling. It was still dark outside but something told him to arise. He crawled from his sleeping bag and down from the hayloft. As Gregory walked through the milk house he noticed that John's herd was already standing in line at the door. It was like someone had herded them there, but how could that be? Gregory was

the only one there. The thought entered his mind,
"Lay hands on the head of each animal and say,
'Bring forth, in the name of Jesus.'" Gregory
thought, "That's crazy," and decided to go back to
sleep.

As he was climbing the ladder to the loft his
heart raced and it felt like he was having a heart
attack. He climbed back down and his heart beat
returned to normal. He tried to climb the ladder
again but his heart raced once more. After climbing
down his heart returned to normal once again.

Gregory spoke out loud, "Lord! What is it you
want from me?"

Again, the thought entered his mind, "Lay hands
on the head of each animal and say, "Bring forth, in
the name of Jesus."

Gregory shouted, "All 166?"

After several minutes of wrestling with his
thoughts he returned to the milk house to find all the
cows still standing outside the door. Gregory spent
the next few hours praying over each animal as
instructed. Gregory was captivated by all this.
Every cow quietly stood in line and when Gregory
finished his prayer over that particular animal it
walked away, back to pasture.

Gregory prayed over the last animal then he
went back to bed.

John woke Gregory up around eight the next
morning. While shaking Greg, John said
excitedly, "Get up, something incredible as
happened!"

"What is it?"

"Get up! Hurry!"

John stood in the barn lot staring in amazement. While rubbing his eyes, Gregory said, "What is it?"

"Look!"

There were several milk transport trucks sitting in the driveway.

"What are they doing here?" Gregory asked.

"Something incredible has happened! I started the milking this morning and they won't stop!"

"I don't understand." Gregory replied.

"The cows! They won't stop giving milk! It's incredible, man!"

Gregory kept his thoughts to himself, but inside he was jumping for joy. He just nodded his head, "Yeah, it is!"

Gregory soon packed his belongings and started walking down the drive.

Julie yelled from the house, "You're leaving?" Julie ran to where Gregory was standing.

"I'm afraid so," he said.

John walked over to his wife and Gregory. With a tearful eye he extended his hand. "Thanks for walking down our path, son."

"Don't worry about the bank, John. God won't turn off the faucet till the mortgage is paid."

John looked at Gregory with a puzzled grin. Julie grabbed Gregory and hugged him. After a few moments she pushed him away and wiped the tears from her eyes.

John said, "Good luck, son." as he and Gregory shook hands to say goodbye.

He found his way back to State Road 31 and then made his way over to Interstate 70.

While traveling 70, he made stops in Acme, Craysville, and Allenport along the Ohio river.

With a little over three hundred miles of Pennsylvania under his belt and 26 days of road behind him, it came time to cross over into West Virginia. Gregory made another stop at an ATM before the border into Ohio. He made the following entry into his journal after entering the Buckeye state.

"April 17."

"I was walking along 40 yesterday near Roneys Point, West Virginia. An Amish horse and buggy pulled up beside me and stopped. The gentleman inside asked if I wanted a ride, I declined. I thought, how strange it was to see Amish in the hills of West Virginia. The Amish man told me to cleanse my soul because many would look to me. He also said to not be afraid of what was to come. I stood there stunned, how did he know that? They started to trot away. I ran as hard as I could to catch up. While running beside the buggy, I yelled, 'What's your name?' He said, 'Gabe.' I stopped running to ponder what just happened. As I stood in the middle of the road, I watched that horse and buggy disappear before my very eyes.

"<u>That was an angel!</u>"

No More

The carved wooden sign said, "Welcome to Barkcamp State Park." Gregory noticed the park he had wandered into had an adjacent lake. He decided to check out what the locals called "Belmont Lake." It was late, he was tired, and he didn't feel much like going through the procedure of checking into the campgrounds. He made his way down to the lakeshore and decided to make camp behind some cattails. Gregory was so worn out that he didn't even bother making a fire, he just curled up in his sleeping bag hoping for a good night's sleep. Little did he know trouble was about to come knocking.

Gregory awoke to the sounds of screaming. He climbed out of his sleeping bag to peer through the cattails. He witnessed, what he thought, was a rape. On the other side of the lake, he saw what appeared to be a red mustang, parked, with the engine running. On the ground beside the car, two boys were holding a girl down while another guy was raping her. What he witnessed next horrified him. The girl managed to break one arm free. She then scratched the attacker across the face with her fingernails. The guy on top of her grabbed his face, then he grabbed a rock. Gregory stood and watched in disbelief. Quite angry, the attacker beat her to death with the rock. Gregory thought to himself, "I just witnessed a murder!" It happened so fast.

He thought to himself, "I've got to do something!" He stood up and yelled, "Stop!" The boys ran in a panic. They jumped in the car and sped off. Gregory ran to the other side of the lake. There she was. He knelt down beside her, placed a finger to her neck and checked for a pulse, there was none. He tried CPR, but it was in vain. He shouted, "Lord, help me raise this girl!"

Gregory shook her shoulders as he said, "I command the spirit of life back into you, in the name of Jesus!" He repeated those words several times, but to no avail. He sat back, brought his knees to his face and began to weep. He just sat there, staring at her. She was a cheerleader, still dressed in her uniform. The label on her chest said, "Hi, I'm Katie." An attractive girl with blond hair soaked with the blood from her head wound.

After quite some time Gregory decided he had to report this. He gathered up her lifeless body, held her in his arms, and started walking towards the park entrance.

The boys fled to nearby Clarisville. The driver, with his face bleeding, drove straight to the Sheriff's department. He jumped out of the car and told the other two to stay put. As he walked through the front door he shouted, "Where's my uncle?"

The deputy replied by saying, "What happened to your face, Will?"

"Is my uncle here?"

"He's in his office."

Will stormed into the Sheriff's office and slammed the door behind himself. Placing both hands on the desk he said, "I'm in trouble Uncle Tom."

"What happened to your face?"

"I think I killed someone tonight."

"Have you been drinkin'?

"We drank a few."

"Now calm down son, tell me what happened."

"You see, me and Eddie and Chuck were just out celebratin' cause Belmont won the game and all. We drove around for awhile, drank a few beers, then Chuck decided he wanted to pick up his girlfriend. We saw her friend's car at the Pizza Hut. We walked in and told the other cheerleaders we'd give her a ride home. After we all drank a twelve pack, Chuck decides he wants to go to the lake. On the way, Chuck's girlfriend passes out in the back seat, you see. He told me to look in the rear view mirror. He pulled her pants down and raised her dress. He told me if I wanted some of that, it was alright with him. We got to the lake and I parked the car. Chuck pushed her out the door and I got on top of her while they watched. She must not have been to drunk because she woke up. I told Chuck and Eddie to hold her while I got some, and before I knew it she scratched me."

"Then what happened, Will?"

"I got mad and hit her with a rock. I'm so sorry Uncle Tom."

"Now don't you worry about a thing. You and your buddies go on home now, ya hear?"

As Will walked for the door, Sheriff Tom placed a hand on his shoulder.

"And Will."

"Yeah."

"Don't breath a word of this to anyone, okay?"

"Okay."

The sheriff followed Will out the door and past the front desk. He told the deputy in passing that he would be back, he's taking a ride to the lake.   The Sheriff jumped into his squad car and drove. A short time later, he passed the entrance to the park. He slammed on the brakes when he saw Gregory carrying the dead girl's body along side the road. The sheriff opened the door of his squad car, and with pistol drawn, yelled, "Police, put the girl down!"

"She's dead. Three boys killed her." Gregory shouted.

"I said, put the girl down!"

"I tried to save her!"

"Put the girl down or I'll shoot! Do it now!"

Gregory hesitated.

"Now!"

Gregory laid the girl down gently. With pistol still drawn, the Sheriff slowly walked over to Gregory.

"Hands behind your head!"

Gregory hesitated again.

"Do it now!"

The Sheriff checked for weapons and then ordered Gregory to place his hands behind his back. Before handcuffing him, the Sheriff had Gregory pick the girl up and put her in the back seat of the squad car. As Gregory was laying her on the seat the Sheriff had his gun pointed at Gregory's head.

"You make one wrong move! Turn around slowly, and put these cuffs on."

Gregory had no choice but to comply.

"Get in the front seat."

With gun still drawn and pointed at Gregory, the Sheriff slid into the driver's seat.

"Now, take me to where you murdered her."

"I didn't kill her, I told ya that."

"Shut up! Which way?"

Gregory pointed to the direction of the lake. Once there, the Sheriff told Gregory to grab a rock.

"That's evidence Jack, and your prints are all over it."

"That's not the rock he used."

"Get in the car!"

"Where are we going?"

"You're goin' to jail!"

"What about my stuff?"

"What stuff?"

"My things."

"You campin' here?"

"Yeah, why?"

"Anybody see ya?"

"No, just those guys who killed her!"

"There were no guys, now move! Show me that stuff of yours."

Gregory led the Sheriff to his camp site. The Sheriff gathered all of Gregory's belongings and put them in the trunk of the squad car. He drove his prisoner to the Belmont County Jail, booked him, and placed him in a private cell.

Gregory woke in the morning to the sound of a key turning in the cell door.

"Get up boy! It's 9 and you got some explaining to do."

The deputy led Gregory to a room down the hall.

"Have a seat, the Sheriff wants to have a word with ya."

The deputy left Gregory sitting alone in a room that had mirrors on all four walls.   After a few moments the Sheriff walked in and sat down across from his prisoner.

"I'm Sheriff Tom McCants." He said, "Cigarette?" as he lit one up and took a drag.

"I don't smoke."

The Sheriff then blew smoke in Gregory's face.

"Now, why don't you make things easy and just tell us why you killed her."

"I told you, I didn't kill her!"

"I know. It was three guys! How'd they get there genius?"

"A car! A red one, Mustang, I think!"

"There weren't any tire tracks there genius!"

"I seen it. I'm tellin' ya, I seen it!"

Gregory wasn't aware that the Sheriff rubbed the tire tracks out during the early morning hours.

The Sheriff leaned into Gregory's face.

"I'm sick of your lies! Now tell me what I wanna know."

"I want a lawyer!"

"He's out of town."

"I'm not saying anything till I speak with a lawyer."

The Sheriff paced around the small room.

"You know who you killed?"

Gregory hung his head and stared at the floor in silence.

"Her name was Katie Lynn Rogers. She was a cheerleader at Belmont High School. A straight A student, only 15. A good girl, and you killed her!"

Gregory said nothing.

"I know all about you, pal!"

Gregory looked over at the Sheriff.

"You got busted for a DUI, didn't ya?"

Gregory stared at the Sheriff in silence.

"You got a record, Matthews!"

"How did you know my name? I never gave you my name!"

"Ever heard of fingerprints?"

As the Sheriff looked through his papers, he stated, "I know all about you! Your name, age, everything!"

"What is it you want Sheriff?"

"Well, let's see."

The Sheriff pulled Gregory's backpack from a wall locker and dumped the contents on the table.

Gregory jumped up and said, "That's my stuff!"

"It's evidence, pal!"

Gregory sat back down.

The Sheriff picked up each item as he examined it.

"Oh … a Bible! You're one of them!"

"One what?"

"Jesus freak!"

Getting quite mad and red in the face, Sheriff Tom slid his chair over to where Gregory's was.

He got right up in Gregory's face.

"My old man was just like you."

Gregory leaned back and said, "Like what?"

"A religious freak! He was a pastor at the local church and he dragged me there every Sunday. There was one problem, he was a freakin' fraud! He banged the piano player during the week, drank, and told Mom he repented on Sunday. Your type makes me sick!"

"I'm not your dad."

"Shut up! You're goin' back to holding."

The Sheriff walked out the door, but it didn't completely close. Gregory panicked. He threw his belongings into the backpack and decided to run. Walking down the hall he saw a window cracked open. He slid a chair under the window, threw his backpack out, and climbed through the opening to freedom. After a few moments, the Sheriff returned to discover his prisoner had escaped. Within short order, the Sheriff issued an APB. (All points bulletin) It hit the Teletype and police band air waves, but it was too late. Gregory was long gone by now.

Gregory was a wanted man now, a fugitive. He remembered watching that series on television in the 60's, but he never dreamed he'd become one. In the days to come, he would lay low and travel at night. He was a man on the run with a cry in his heart of, "Lord, is this the best you have for me?"

Gregory knew he made a mistake by running, but he never realized that Sheriff Tom was setting him up for the murder of Katie Rogers. Seeing that the evidence pointed in his direction, he simply concluded that the Sheriff didn't buy his story. He didn't know that the good Sheriff had stacked the cards. Tom left the door and window cracked open on purpose. He wanted Gregory to escape! The Sheriff's mindset was one of if Gregory got killed his nephew would be off the hook. After all, his kind deserves to die.

Scared to travel during the day, thinking someone would recognize him, Gregory began to travel under the cover of darkness. It became a necessity. He spent his first day on the run living in a cardboard box on the street. Nobody pays attention to the homeless. An excellent way to blend in, he thought. He had become the person he ignored on Wall Street, and that left him with a sick feeling in the pit of his stomach.

Traveling at night was slow, but he needed to act on the side of caution. The back roads were now the main agenda.   He would document his tremendous fear in the archives of that journal. He wrote of a day spent under the leaves in a woods near Norwich, off 40. Another day on 40, near Hebron, found him hiding in an abandon house. New Hope, close to 35, had a broken down barn that was quite inviting. One of the more unusual places he chose was in the top of a billboard across the street from the Enon package liquor store. Nobody pays attention to drunks either, became his reasoning.

He also wrote of his experience at Lake Madison, a state park near Lilly Capel. "I stayed in the reeds today, near the lake. I'm too scared to try the campgrounds. Why is this happening to me?

I'm innocent! Lord, is this how you repay your followers?

Before I left that night, I got surprised by a fishermen. He was fishing for catfish and lost control of his boat. He rammed the reeds where I was hiding. He got a real good look at me! I think I startled him more than he did me. He asked me why I didn't have a fire started and the reason why I wasn't in the campground. I lied and said my matches were wet and I liked roughing it. I think he bought it because he threw me a book of matches and told me it was illegal to camp anywhere that wasn't designated in the park. I told him thanks and that I would pack up and head over to the campground. I lied about that, too. I headed down the road after he was out of sight. I regret the lies!

Before he left, the fishermen told me to be careful. I acted naive and played dumb. He said he read in the Columbus Dispatch that there was a killer on the loose. The dead girl is that editor's niece! As the fisherman put it, that editor is a reporter with a mission now. He wants justice.

<u>That's all I need, press!</u>"

Gregory would eventually manage to make it to the Indiana line. Two hundred and fifty miles of Ohio back roads were behind him, but it had taken nineteen days. He was now a federal fugitive, he crossed state lines. The date: May 6th.

Deception

Only a few miles inside the Hoosier state line, and a stone's throw away from Chester, the sun was beginning to come up. Searching for a place to hide, Gregory got startled by the blinding headlights that crested the hill. Talking to himself he said, "Don't run!" As the car drew closer, terror laid its claim. Gregory quickly threw his backpack in the ditch. As the car slowed, Gregory recognized it to be a police cruiser. His hands, now sweaty, quickly went into his pockets. The officer stopped, shined his spotlight on him, and rolled down the window.

"Trouble?" The officer asked.

"No."

"What are you doing out here, son?"

"Just out for a morning jog."

"You should wait till the sun comes up a little more before you do that, or wear some type of reflective tape. Drivers can't see you in the dark. Well … enjoy your run."

"Thanks for the tip, officer."

"Be safe, have a good day."

"Thank you."

While the officer was driving away, Gregory faked resuming a morning run. As soon as the cruiser disappeared from sight, Gregory turned around and ran back to the ditch to retrieve his backpack.

A short time later, Sheriff Burns pulled into the jail parking lot and made his way to the office. Sitting at his desk with head down, he shouted out a profanity.

The desk clerk, startled by what she heard, ran into the sheriff's office to say, "Sheriff, are you all right?"

Waving a piece of paper over his head, he shouted, "When did we get this?" A disgusted tone in his voice expressed his anger.

"What is it? The female officer inquired.

"Its a freakin' APB for murder, that's what it is!"

"It came in over the Teletype last night, why?"

"I let him slip right through my fingers this morning, that's why! Get on the horn. Send Larry and Ed over to Ford road. Give em' the description and tell em' to be careful, he's wanted for murder. Great, I would imagine he's long gone by now though."

Sheriff Burns slammed his fist on the desk then he dialed the phone. A call went into the FBI's field office in Indianapolis.

"Hello, Federal Bureau of Investigation, may I help you?"

"This is Sheriff Burns … Wayne County … I need to talk to one of your agents."

"Just a moment, Sir." The operator added.

After a minute or two someone answered the phone to say, "This is agent Winn, can I help you?"

With a listening ear, agent Winn documented everything Sheriff Burns had to share about the fugitive's sighting. Agent Larry Winn, a veteran of twenty years, would be later assigned to the case as its lead investigator. He, and two other agents, in time, would travel to Wayne County and then to Belmont County in Ohio to seek evidence for the building of their case.

From the time Gregory escaped, his days on the run would become filled with loneliness and boredom. He would sleep with one eye open, so to speak, and one on his Bible. God's word was a constant companion now. To pass the time, he read daily. Although he highlighted Psalm 27:1, he hadn't quite yet believed its entire truth.

Now near Jacksonburg, Gregory sought refuge in the Martindale State Fishing area. A gentle rain began to fall that morning. Cold and wet, Gregory decided to take shelter under a nearby bridge. Gathering driftwood, that had been cast ashore, became the next task. Among the large rocks, he built a small fire to dry himself, his belongings, and warm his chilled bones. "Great, nobody's fishin' in the rain today." He thought.

He dumped the backpack out. Provisions being low, only a can of beans fell to the ground. His wallet, moisture steaming from it from the heat of the fire, fell off the rock it was laying on. Gregory reached down to pick it up. Still quite warm, he opened it. Two dollars fell to the ground. In disgust, he kicked them. Gregory then raised his knees to his face. While sitting on a large rock he began to weep, then cry out.

"God! Why is this happening to me? I didn't kill anybody! I can't see any glory in this! I'm broke,

I'm scared, and I'm hungry. If you're really there, help me!"

Moments later, the stream's water in front of him began to swirl. A small whirlpool developed. Suddenly, a large fish jumped from the whirlpool to the bank only a few inches away. It flopped two or three times. When its gills stopped moving, Gregory looked to the sky and winked.

"Dinner!" He laughed.

Curiously, Gregory poked the fish with a stick. Something was hanging from the corner of its mouth. He reached down to pull it from the jaws of the creature. Gregory leaned back with amazement at his discovery. He began to weep with gratitude. The fish had swallowed a crisp one hundred dollar bill that had been wrapped in plastic. Perfectly dry, he thought a fishermen must have lost it some how.

Dry by now, with a full stomach and money in his pocket, he decided on a nap before hitting the road again. Gregory read a few verses and said a prayer before catching some much needed winks. "Lord, thanks! I'm sorry about the outburst earlier."

Later on that night, in the early morning hours, Gregory would put the much needed miracle funds to good use. Considering it to be too risky, Gregory elected to bypass Interstate 70 that passed through the heart of Indianapolis. Traveling Old 52, Gregory made his way into New Palestine and its convenience store. The sign on the front door said, "We can't take 50's or 100's!" Pulling the bill out of his pocket to demonstrate, Gregory told the clerk he was hungry and that's all he had. She smiled and made an exception.

Leaving the store, Gregory couldn't forget the song the PA system had been playing while he shopped. It was Willie Nelson's hit, "Back on the road again." It remained several hours in the playback mode of his mind.

Three or four days later he spent another rainy day hiding away in a kid's abandoned tree house, one not far from the White River, near Stones Crossing.

One morning, while walking in the early morning fog on 142 near Eminence, Gregory heard a terrible sound. A car had just passed him in the southbound lane. He was walking along the edge of the road, the driver obviously hadn't seen Gregory and missed hitting him by only inches. Gregory thought to himself, "That guy's goin' way too fast in that fog." Running to the sound, Gregory stumbled upon a horrifying scene.

Dropping his backpack, Gregory ran to the cars. They had hit head-on. The first vehicle, the one that just passed him, was broken into pieces. Inside the wreckage, the dismembered body of a man lay. It was obvious, death had called. "Oh, Lord," Gregory whispered. The sight gagged him.

He could hear moaning coming from the other vehicle. Gregory ran to find an injured woman slumped over the steering wheel of the other car, it too being badly damaged. He touched her neck with his fingers to check for a pulse. With a deep moan, she fell backward in her seat. "Just take it easy now. My name's Greg, help's on its way." Bleeding from the head, she uttered with a moan,

"My boy." Gregory tore a sleeve from his jacket
and wrapped it around her head.

Gregory quickly did a visual scan of the vehicle's
interior. There was no one else in the vehicle, just
her. "There's no sign of him," he thought. He
noticed the passenger door was missing. It had been
ripped off along with the seatbelt harness. Gregory
began to walk the perimeter of the crash site. He
discovered a young boy's body lying on the
pavement only a few yards away. Unconscious, he
appeared to be only three or four years old. "He
doesn't have a scratch on him!" Gregory thought.

Touching the boy's neck, Gregory could tell he
was gone.

With a frantic tone, a voice from behind said,
"Jimmy!" The injured woman had made her way
out of the wreckage and over to where Gregory was
kneeling. Dropping to her knees, she grabbed her
son around the neck and held him to her chest.
Crying, she said, "Oh … God … no!"

Within a matter of moments, someone else was
standing over them, a farmer, dressed in
overalls.

"I blocked the road. What can I do?" He asked.

Gregory asked if he had a cell phone.

"Yes, I got one."

"Call 911 then."

"I already did."

"That's good."

"They should be here anytime." The farmer
added.

Gregory looked up at the man and nodded his head in silence. Touching the woman on the shoulder, Gregory said, "Let me try."

Thinking Gregory wanted to try CPR, she released the hold on her son. With the boy lying on his back, motionless, Gregory laid his hands on his chest. Closing his eyes and looking to the sky, Gregory shouted, "I command the spirit of life back into you, in the name of Jesus!" After a moment of silence, nothing seemed to be happening. Gregory repeated the cry. Again, nothing seemed to happen. He repeated it for the third time, then the boy coughed. The farmer and mother looked on as the boy awoke. He sat up to say, "Mommy, where am I?"

The mother rushed to embrace her son with the farmer right behind. With sirens approaching in the distance, Gregory slipped from their presence. He disappeared into the mist under the fog's cover. Walking away, Gregory questioned God. "Why that boy … and not the cheerleader?"

After a brief moment of crying, mixed with laughter, the farmer turned to say, "That sure was somethin' mister." Surprised, he didn't realize Gregory had left. An ambulance soon arrived along with the police. The officer's report would later read: "One dead, one injured. Witnesses state, an angel raised the dead on 142 this day."

Zig-zagging through the countryside was starting to become a habit. Avoiding detection was foremost on Gregory's mind. The night's route was Indiana State Road 42. It led past the southern tip of Cataract Lake. Lieber State Park bordered the lake to the north and he noticed a rather inviting sign. By the light of the moon, Gregory made his way along the half mile tract. With the falls ahead, he thought, "Shower!"

Gregory stood to gather in the visual beauty of the falls. He thought to himself, "You sure do have a creative hand, Lord." After he made his way to the back of the falls, he got undressed. With a bar of soap in hand, he spent the next hour enjoying the cool sensation of water flowing over his body. The sun was starting to peer through the trees, dawn was coming. Gregory figured that hole in the wall behind the falls would be the perfect hiding spot.

Sleeping almost all day, Gregory woke late afternoon to the sounds of children playing. Only yards away, families were enjoying their day together in the picnic area. Watching until the sun disappeared over the horizon, he began to analyze the missing pieces of his life. Gregory would continue to travel 42 until reaching the state line.

A couple days before he crossed over into Illinois, Gregory had heard some news. Spending the day not too far from Youngstown, along that river called the Wabash, Gregory slept under a row boat. It lay upside down on the bank. It was the perfect hiding place, assuming no one used it that day.

Gregory woke to the sounds of a radio that day. A fishermen downstream had tuned into the local station. Gregory raised the boat's edge slightly with his fingers and placed a rock under it. He listened intently. The broadcast was soon interrupted for a news bulletin. The announcer told of a FBI man hunt. Clearing his throat, the announcer spoke:

"Local authorities, along with the FBI, are on the lookout for a murder suspect. They warn he may be in the area. His name is Gregory Ian Matthews. He's 34, has blue eyes, brown hair, and stands five feet ten inches tall. He's been known to carry a backpack and is considered quite dangerous. If you witness anything suspicious, or see anyone that matches that description, please report it to the local authorities. Don't attempt capture. This has been a WKLB special news report."

Gregory removed the rock and lowered the boat. In the darkness, Gregory whispered, "I'm in big trouble, Lord."

Wonder

The next evening, while leaning against a fence post, Gregory unfolded the journal to write:

"May 26."

"It's getting lonely out here. Being on the run isn't much fun. In Illinois now. I put two hundred fearful miles of Indiana behind me tonight. Praying, but getting no answers. I wish I knew His plan. I'm scared."

Agent Winn and his team, traveling to Chester, Indiana the day before, were now on their way to investigate in Ohio.   The Wayne County Sheriff wasn't much help to the FBI agents. He recalled his conversation with Gregory, but didn't remember seeing a backpack. The Sheriff couldn't really determine which direction he was headed either.

At the crack of dawn, a black sedan rolled into St. Clairsville.

"Guys, let's pay the Belmont County Sheriff a visit first. What do ya say?" Agent Winn suggested.

The other two nodded in agreement.

After walking through the front door, all three showed their credentials to the desk clerk.

"I'm agent Winn."

Pointing to his fellow agents, Winn said, "This is agent Smith and Sutherland. We'd like to talk to the Sheriff."

"He hasn't showed up yet, but he should be along anytime" the clerk answered.

"We'll wait" said Winn.

Two hours later, the Sheriff walked through the door. Obviously in a bad mood, he looked at the agents and then to the clerk. Sheriff McCants then shouted, "Who are these people?"

Agent Winn jumped to his feet and pulled out his credentials. "We need a moment of your time, Sheriff. I'm agent Winn, lead investigator. These are agents Smith and Sutherland. We're with the FBI."

Sheriff McCants replied with, "Can't you see I'm busy."

Agent Winn countered with, "You don't look that busy to me, Sir."

"Read my report. Now get out!"

That infuriated Winn and he threw Sheriff McCants against the wall. With a hand full of McCants's collar, Winn pressed his nose to the Sheriff's face.

"We didn't drive down here for nothin'. You're goin' to tell us what we want to know."

Agent Winn walked the Sheriff over to his office and shoved him into a chair. McCants then cleared his throat to say, "What can I do for you … Gentlemen?"

Agents Smith and Sutherland sat in chairs across from the Sheriff. Winn sat on the corner of the desk and pulled out a notebook.

With a worried look on his face, the Sheriff stated he had already reported the matter.

"That's interesting. How do you know what we're here for?"

Agent Winn looked across at the other two and they nodded.

"Well, it's a small town. I assumed you were here for the murder."

"I see." Winn replied. "We read the report, Sheriff. And yes, we're investigating the Katie Lynn Rogers murder. That's funny you would assume that."

Winn looked to his fellow agents once more, and they winked.

Sheriff McCants leaned back in his chair and placed his hands behind his head. He said, "Don't you think it's overkill for the government to assign three of you to this?"

Winn, in turn, kicked McCants's chair.

"We're takin' this investigation over. I'll ask the questions … you answer."

McCants leaned forward to clear his throat once more. With pen and notebook in hand, Winn began.

"The victim was Katie Lynn Rogers. A local girl … correct?"

McCants looked down to say, "A cheerleader. That's right."

"How was the crime reported?"

McCants raised his head to stare at Winn. "It's in the report!"

"Tell me again." Winn asked.

"Three boys from town were at the lake that night and witnessed it. They told me about it, then I drove out there and caught the guy."

"Just like that?"

Staring once more at the agent, McCants said, "Just like that!"

Winn looked over at his partners. They leaned forward in their chairs as to listen more closely.

"The report said the suspect was apprehended at the entrance to the park, is that right?"

"Right!"

"I don't understand somethin'. Why would the guy just be walkin' down the road with a dead girl in his arms? And you just happened to be driving by when you saw him … right?"

Getting angry, McCants countered with, "Am I the one who's on trial here? I don't know what the guy was thinkin'. Maybe he was tryin' to bury her."

Winn closed his book and said, "Sheriff, it's been nice talking to ya. We'll keep in touch."

As they walked out the door, Smith looked to agent Winn and said, "What do you think?"

Winn looked to Sutherland and said, "What do you think?"

Sutherland said, "It don't add up. I think he's lyin'."

Winn answered, "Me too. Let's take a trip to the high school."

Using the principal's office, the agents interviewed Katie Lynn Rogers's friends one at a time. After they finished the interviews, they paid the local diner a visit to go over their notes over a cup of coffee.

Winn pulled out his notebook as the three sat. Smith and Sutherland pulled out theirs.

"This whole thing smells." Winn stated in a raised tone of voice.

"Why would the guy be walking down the road with a dead girl in his arms?" Sutherland asked.

Winn asked Smith, "What's your take on it, Steve?

Holding a cup of coffee in front of him while running his fingers around the rim, Smith said, "Let's say a guy murders a girl. One, he may leave the body as a trophy for us to find."

Sutherland added, "If he's mental!"

Smith continued with, "Two, he may panic and leave it."

Winn said, "Go on."

"Three, he buries the body. Or Four, he's just nuts and likes to walk around with dead bodies."

Winn replied, "Doesn't fit, does it?"

Smith added, "Or he may be lookin' for help."

Sutherland countered with, "Remember what those cheerleaders said?"

Winn and Smith listened with intent.

"All four had the same story, guys. They saw the girl leave Pizza Hut with the boys that night. That wasn't in the Sheriff's report … remember?"

Winn said, "Interesting … go on."

"One of the girls said the Sheriff's nephew had a bandage on his face in class the next day. All four said his face looked normal at Pizza Hut!"

"You buy that dog scratching his face story?" Winn asked.

"No." Sutherland replied.

"Well, all three boys said they seen Matthews kill her at the lake." Winn said.

"Didn't you think the boys acted nervous around us?" Smith asked.

"Yeah." Sutherland replied.

Winn injected, "I don't like what I'm hearing, but we need more."

Smith said, "All we got is a rock with her blood on it and Matthews fingerprints."

Sutherland said, "I smell a rat."

Winn ended the conversation with, "We need Gregory Matthews."

Before leaving the diner, Smith looked at Winn and said, "You know that little deal back there at the Sheriff's office? You roughing him up and all?"

"What about it?" Winn asked.

"I'm goin' have to report that when we get back home." After thinking about it for a moment, Smith commented, "Well … maybe I won't."

A few days later, Gregory was perched atop a cliff near the Lincoln Trail State Park. Not being able to sleep that day, he read Psalms. The entire book of Psalms, as a matter of fact. Sitting on a rock, with a cliff for a backdrop, he stared at the roots that openly dangled from above. "I'm like that!" He thought. "On the run, and can't put down roots." Holding his Bible in the air, Gregory shouted, "I never realized how much you had to say in this thing before." In a humble tone, he said: "Thanks for the book, Lord, thanks for the light." Gregory then began to weep.

Still traveling by night, Gregory made his way down from the Lincoln Trail and Westward. Urged by necessity, he endeavored to travel light and fast. It was a hot one, the last night of May. Gregory could see the dim lights of Heartville to the north. It was a vast distance, but unseemingly so to the untrained eye. A dirt road that connected 19 to 45 would be his inconspicuous mode of travel for the evening, but destiny was about to play the card of fate that night, and Gregory was about to play right into its hand.

Several yards up the road, he could see the moonlit silhouette of a vehicle parked in the middle of the road. He could hear screams coming from that direction. He dropped his backpack and ran that way. The rusted out Chevy would hold many a surprise.

Gregory opened the door and found a Hispanic lady lying across the front seat.   It was quite obvious, she was having a baby.   Every time a contraction came, she screamed. Gregory didn't know much about delivering babies, but he knew this one was on its way. He knew it wouldn't be long because her water was broken, most of it being on the floorboard. He was in the delivery room when "L" was born, but that surely didn't make him an expert. Bending her knees, then spreading her legs, she pulled her dress up. Gregory got a real good look at what was going on down there!

He stared at her to say, "Oh … boy!"

That being the first spoken words between the two, she countered with Spanish.

She screamed, then said, "Es usted un angel?"

Looking puzzled, Gregory said nothing.

She screamed again, saying, "Es usted un angel?" once more.

Gregory said, "I don't understand!"

She repeated the phrase again.

"Es usted un angel?"

Thinking it would calm her down, and not knowing how to speak Spanish, Gregory just nodded his head. He had no idea that she was asking if he were an angel.   It worked, she calmed down dramatically.

After that, she would repeatedly say, "Gracias, Jesus!"

Gregory didn't know what that meant either, but in reality she was simply saying, "Thank you, Jesus!"

The baby was coming and the screams intensified.

"I can see the head!"   Gregory shouted.

"Gracias, Jesus!" was her reply.

Rolling up his sleeves, Gregory bent over with arms extended in preparation for the delivery. The miracle of life was about to occur.

"It's a boy!"   Gregory shouted.

"Gracias, Jesus!" She then whispered.

Holding him, Gregory just stared at the boy. He looked to the mother and smiled. She smiled with a sigh of relief.

Gregory looked at the mother and said, "I wish I could understand you."

With a smile, she said nothing.

Gregory looked to the boy once more and said, "Birth is a wonder, but being born again is truly a miracle."

Gregory removed his shirt and wrapped it around the child. With cord still connected, he laid the child on her stomach. She immediately wrapped her arms around the baby and began to weep.

Suddenly, the glare of approaching headlights flooded the vehicle's interior. In a panic, Gregory ran for the ditch and the field nearby. He hid on his stomach in the knee high corn. Watching and listening intently, he remained motionless. A truck pulled in behind the car and stopped. A man, dressed in overalls, exited the driver's side and walked over to the car.

With an urgent tone, he yelled, "Honey! Honey, come here!"

"What is it Ralph?" She yelled from the truck window.

"Get over here … now!"

The woman jumped from the vehicle and ran to where her husband was standing.

"I don't think she understands English, sweetheart. She won't answer me."

"She just had a baby, Ralph!"

"I can see that!"

"We need to get her to the hospital."

"It's a good thing you're a nurse, sweetheart."

"I know."

She leaned into the car to check mother and baby.

Ralph said, "I wonder why she's clear out here, in the middle of nowhere? Nobody travels this old farm road at night."

"You got the cell phone with you, Ralph?"

"Yeah. Yeah, I do."

"Call 911 and tell them where we are."

Dialing the numbers, the farmer told his wife, "You know something?"

"What?"

"That lady's real lucky."

"Why?"

"Well … what's the odds of us coming down this road, at this time of night, and you being a nurse? And on top of all that, the hospital only being ten miles from here and this being your first night switching to this shift."

"Odd, isn't it?"

"No, I think it's a whole lot more than that."

An ambulance arrived several minutes later and the nurse decided to ride to work in the ambulance with the mother and her baby.

"Driver, my name's Ann Shore, I'm the third shift charge nurse on 2A at Effingham General. That's where you're taking her, right?"

"Yeah."

"Can I get a lift to work?"

"Sure, jump in!"

"Ann, are you sure you don't want me to go along?" Ralph asked.

"No, sweetheart. She'll be fine. I'll grab a ride with these guys and I'll see you in the morning."

"You sure?"

"Yeah, I'm sure. You go on home now."

Ralph kissed his wife goodbye, then jumped back in their truck. In opposite directions, the ambulance pulled away and so did he. Gregory waited for everyone to leave before he emerged from hiding, then he searched for his backpack. After he found it, he threw it over his shoulder and got back out on the road again. "That was cool how you did that, Lord!" Gregory said, while looking to the sky.

Gregory was becoming quite clever at finding places to hide. Before he entered the *"Show Me"* state, he wrote in his journal about hiding in an abandoned sawmill near St. Jacob. He also told of a day spent in an old World War II duce and a half. From the many nights of watching the history channel, he recognized it to be a troop transport truck. Stuck in the Kaskaskia River bank mud, near Vera, it was the perfect place to hide.

He would also write the following:

"June 13."

"One hundred and fifty more miles down and eighteen more days gone. I can see the Missouri border from where I sit, it's about a mile or so away. I'll cross tonight. I think it would be a good idea to spend the day in prayer."

Although Gregory said many prayers that day, he repeated one in particular many times.

"Lord, I pray the real killer will be brought to justice."

The Source

Gregory crossed into Missouri that night and it brought back many memories. The time passed quickly because his thoughts were consumed with that of his childhood. He never did quite figure out why they called it the "Show Me" state, he knew it had something to do with a donkey though. He also thought it was odd that most of the roads were lettered and not numbered. Most memorable to him were the times at his father's cabin on *Lake of the Ozarks*. He would later attribute those experiences to his love of the water.

A flood of memories was his companion that evening, but that was coming to an end with the rising of the sun. Near West Alton, at the mouth of the Missouri River, a hydroelectric dam lay ahead. He noticed a feeder pipe that ran from the back of the dam. It emptied into the creek below. With "No trespassing" signs posted everywhere, he thought it a safe bet. "No one will look in there!" He thought.

The pipe looked to be used for overflow and as Gregory stared inside, he visually estimated it to be about eight feet in diameter. Earlier, Gregory tripped over two boards that were wedged in the rocks below, they now caught his eye. Freeing the timbers, Gregory dragged them and himself into the new hideout. Crawling to the back of the pipe, where the absence of light prevailed, he wedged the timber into the pipe's walls. Catching up on some much needed rest, Gregory spent the rest of the day sleeping above the water that trickled past.

Before departing that evening, Gregory decided to speak with his Creator. "Lord, I'm bored with all this! I'm sick of runnin'. If you get me out of this mess, I promise I will serve you the rest of my days."

Almost immediately, Gregory heard the echo of wings a flutter. Looking to the light at the end of this man-made tunnel, there it was. A dove, basking in the sunlight, was washing itself in the water that was running off the end of the pipe. Watching the bird walk dangerously along the edge, Gregory became engulfed in thought. Was it a sign from the Creator to his servant, and only Gregory could understand its meaning?

Doves symbolized peace to Gregory and he wouldn't kill one for anything, no matter how hungry he was. Looking to the bird, Gregory said, "Livin' on the edge, aren't we?" He then chuckled.

A gentle breeze began to blow, but how could that be? "There's only one open end on this pipe!" He reasoned. It takes two open ends to develop a breeze, or so he thought. Gregory didn't realize it, but the unexplained was about to arrive. The Spirit of God was about to descend upon this man who thought he was alone and in the dark.

Mystified, Gregory saw a fine mist develop from the water below. It began to fill the pipe and his being. In the Bible, he read about how others described the Holy Spirit and what it looked like, but he was never a witness to it. The misty fog, as it was described in ancient times, was now part of Gregory's existence. The experience lasted only a minute or so, but it was life changing. After God's presence left Gregory he wrote the following:

"God smiled on me tonight. He sent the Comforter to, of all places, a drain pipe. Mere words can't describe the tremendous peace that came upon me tonight! I made a promise tonight, and if God keeps his end of the bargain, I'll keep mine."

Over the course of the coming days, that feeling of tremendous peace would hold its mark upon Gregory's soul. Displays of God's awesome power would not subside today or anytime in the immediate future.

Spending the day hidden in the *Chain of Rocks* near St. Paul was once again a day of intense soul searching for Gregory. Reading from Mark, he sowed Jesus's thoughts deeply within himself. Gregory had read His words in chapter sixteen before, but things were much different this time. He was actually starting to believe what he read.

Speaking out loud, while periodically nodding his head, Gregory read, "Go into all the world and preach the good news to all creation. Whoever believes and is baptized will be saved, but whoever does not believe will be condemned. And these signs will accompany those who believe: In my name they will drive out demons; they will speak in new tongues; they will pick up snakes with their hands; and when they drink deadly poison, it will not hurt them at all; they will place their hands on sick people, and they will get well."

Closing his Bible Gregory spoke out, as for God to hear.

"I know you're calling me to your work, Lord. I just wish I knew what it was. I don't know if I'm ready for all this though. I like the idea of laying hands on the sick and them recovering, that's cool, but I can do without the snake bit." Gregory hated snakes; he was quite scared of them.

Speaking again, as for God to hear, Gregory said, "Show me a sign, something so I will know all this will work out."

Several minutes passed and Gregory began to pack his stuff up. The sun was sinking into the horizon when he heard thunder.

"That's odd." He said, while looking to the sky. "There's not a cloud in the sky." Suddenly, out of nowhere, a lightning bolt hit the big oak he was standing under. The sound from that clap of lighting was deafening! He patted his hands all over himself to see if he was okay. "I'm alive!" He shouted.

Hearing the roar of fire, Gregory walked out from under the tree to see what was happening. The top of the tree was definitely on fire, but was it? As Gregory stood and stared, he noticed the branches were burning but they weren't being consumed. The leaves were still green and there wasn't any debris falling. At first he thought, "That's weird," but it didn't take him long to realize God was giving him the sign he asked for. Holding his hands skyward, as to surrender his will, Gregory said, "That's good enough for me, Lord!"

Ever-so-determined, Gregory made his way Westward across the hilly terrain. He spent the following day in one of the many secondary caves of the Graham Cave State Park. He remembered that particular cave from his childhood days. Gregory's father brought him there once. Even now, he could still remember asking the tour guide why the cave was boarded up. He recalled it to be a dangerous one. Much to Gregory's surprise, the cave was still there and the original boards were still hanging over the entrance. He removed a few boards, crawled inside and leaned the boards back over the entrance. "Inconspicuous, that's the name of the game," was his thought.

As a child, Gregory had a favorite activity on Friday night. He never missed "Nightmare Theater" on Channel 4. They showed scary movies and he would curl up to a bowl of popcorn and a blanket to have the wits scared out of him. One particular night they showed a movie called, "Trog." It was about a prehistoric cave man that escaped his confines to enter our world. It killed the innocent people of the town and it gave Gregory nightmares for weeks. Looking around, Gregory thought, "I'm a *troglodyte*!" In a way, he really was because one of the definitions is: "A person of degraded character living in seclusion."

Gregory considered it a relief to leave that place when darkness fell, but inconvenience would take on a whole new meaning, in the form of rain. It rained continually for the next two days and Gregory was ill prepared for it.

The rain came to an end on the third day. It was the break of dawn and just over the hill lay Kingdom City with its population of soon-to-be one hundred and thirteen believers. Gregory saw hundreds, possibly even thousands of vehicles parked in the field below. A large sign advertising the weekend's Flea Market showed the way. Unable to shake the need for shelter, he decided to look for a tent. He would blend right in, or so he thought. Cars were still exiting off Highway E, as he made his way down the hill.

Never really showing interest in that sort of thing before, Gregory scanned through the many booths at a feverish pace. Most of the items for sale were of common nature, but some weren't. With only that tent in mind, Gregory became a man on a mission. He noticed a diverse group of people in attendance that day with not one giving him a second thought. They ranged from the young to the old, the normal and the not so.

Looking at a booth full of antiques, Gregory would soon come to realize his true reason for being there. A silver haired man by the name of Gene Smith was standing beside Gregory. Together, they were looking at the tabled items. Gene said, " Hi," and Gregory nodded. Gene was an elderly man from St. Louis who was on vacation with his wife Linda. Gene had always been in good health, but things were about to dramatically change.

Gene felt the development of pain in his chest that worsened quickly. Grabbing his chest, and Gregory's arm, Gene fell to the ground.

Linda yelled, "Gene!"

Sara, a Features Writer for the *Columbia Daily Tribune* was also on vacation and in attendance that day. From the booth next door, she saw what happened, then ran to the fallen victim. Placing her ear to his chest Sara listened for a heartbeat. There was none. She began CPR, but after several minutes it appeared to be in vain. Gregory feared getting involved, but he couldn't just stand idly by any longer either.

Touching Sara on the shoulder, Gregory said, "Can I try?"

She said, "It's too late."

Gregory removed his backpack and smiled to say, "Please," while he gently pushed her to the side.

With a small crowd gathered, Gregory began to pray under his breath. He placed his hands on Gene's chest and shouted, "I command the spirit of life back into you!" Almost immediately, what felt like surges of electricity began to flow through Gregory's hands into Gene. Gene's body began to shake and convulse. Moments later Gene sat up. Linda shoved Gregory out of the way and hugged her husband.

"Oh, Gene. I thought I lost you."

"God said it wasn't time yet, sweetheart." Gene replied.

With a puzzled look on her face, Linda pushed back from her husband.

"What?"

"God said it wasn't time."

Still having a puzzled look on her face, Linda then turned to Gregory.

"You saved my husband's life. How'd you do that?"

"I didn't do anything." Gregory replied.

"You're a miracle worker, that's what you are."

Getting close to Linda's face, Gregory gently said, "No maam. I'm just the conduit, God's the source!"

Standing up to retrieve his backpack, the crowd stood in silence. As Gregory started to walk away, Sara rushed to his side.

"What's your name stranger? That was incredible back there!"

Gregory said nothing as he continued to walk. Walking at a brisk pace beside him, Sara pulled out a pen and notepad from her purse.

"I'm a reporter with the Columbia paper. I wanna do a story on what just happened back there."

"Not interested," was Gregory's reply.

Sara tried repeatedly to convince him, but it was no use. They had came to the end of the row and Sara stopped, but Gregory kept walking. Never looking back, he disappeared into the horizon while Sara stood and stared.

Gregory walked away without the tent that day, but others walked away with something that logic couldn't explain. Little did they know, God planned it so.

Sara went on to write a story with the headline of: "Modern-Day Moses Visits Flea Market!" The story brought her and the paper much needed notoriety. It hit the Associated Press news wire and was reprinted in newspapers across the country. The story also caught the eye of the FBI.

Following route K, Gregory passed the entrance to *Arron Rock State Park* near Black Water. It was still dark outside and he elected to keep walking. He should have taken that officer's advice back in Indiana. He was afraid to wear reflective tape because that would bring attention, but that also made him hard to see in the dark. As he walked around a curve, Gregory heard the roar of an engine approaching. Not realizing how close the truck was, Gregory stepped to the side. As he rounded the curve a delivery truck driver didn't see Gregory until it was almost too late. Swerving abruptly, the driver missed Gregory by only inches. The driver wanted to stop and give Gregory a piece of his mind, but he thought better of it. Because he was running late, the driver rolled down his window and just shouted an obscenity.

The driver didn't realize it, but a box fell from his truck. By the time Gregory got to where the box fell the driver was long gone. Opening the box, Gregory found a dozen green tarps inside. Taking one, Gregory left the remaining eleven in the box on the side of the road. His line of thinking was, if the driver discovered his loss they would be still lying there upon his return.

Gregory used the tarp that morning to make himself a makeshift pup tent in the woods. He was quite grateful because he got a tent after all. Once more, little did he know, God planned it so.

He hid the next day in a hunter's tree stand near *Sweet Water* along the Black Water River just off 127. He would later write in his journal that it looked like a kid's tree house, but it was quite comfortable.

He would go on to follow State Road Z that led him to the outskirts of *Chapel Hill*. He decided to spend the day in the woods near a pond and railroad tracks. Making camp for the day, but not willing to take a chance on making a fire, Gregory decided to check his provisions. Discovering he was completely out of food, Gregory laid down on his sleeping bag and leaned his back to a rock.

Frustrated, Gregory started talking to himself. "God, I'm hungry! I can't go to the store because I don't have any money. I'm afraid to go to the ATM's too. The FBI no doubt knows about that account by now. I'm starting to feel like Jesse James here. I'm real scared, Lord!"

Bored once more, Gregory cracked open the word. His Bible fell open to Philippians 4:19. He read, "And my God will meet all your needs according to his glorious riches in Christ Jesus." Gregory got quite angry and slammed the book shut.

Shouting at the top of his lungs, Gregory yelled, "What about me? Have you forgotten about me? Or is that promise not for everybody?"

As he sat there stewing, something miraculous began to happen. A squirrel, with a nut in its mouth, ran from the woods and up to Gregory. Only a few inches away, it stood there staring. It stood on its back legs and removed the nut from its mouth then held it in its front paws. Looking puzzled, Gregory held out an open hand. The squirrel crawled over to him, dropped the nut in his hand and ran off. Chuckling, Gregory cracked the gift open on a rock and ate what was inside.

Moments later, another squirrel ran up to Gregory and dropped a nut at his feet. Seconds later, another squirrel did the same thing. Squirrel after squirrel began doing that until hundreds of them had stacked a large pile of nuts in front of him, and just as quick as it started, it ended. Shortly after Gregory realized his visitors were finished with their task, he began to weep. He spent the rest of the day cracking open the meals and asking for God's forgiveness.

The 4th of July was just around the corner, it was the following day, as a matter of fact, and as he rested under a bridge Gregory could hear the pre-celebration fireworks going off in a nearby town. Choosing to bypass Kansas City and avoid the major interstate systems of 470 and 435, he elected to travel the rolling pavement of route Y.

The next evening, Gregory took a big chance. He reasoned that everybody in Belton would be attending the fireworks celebration at the park. He had been watching from afar, but knew it to be a risk. That's the risk his stomach was telling him to take.

Walking up to the Belton State Bank ATM, Gregory attempted to withdraw some money, quickly. Time after time, his attempts failed. The message: "Please contact your service provider," continued to flash across the screen. Disgusted,

Gregory removed his card, all the while thinking the machine was just broken.

Staring across the street, Gregory saw the lights being turned off at *Hap's Place*, a restaurant. He cautiously walked around to the back of the business and waited in the bushes. Before long, the cook exited the building to throw leftovers in the dumpster. After some time, the cook locked the door and drove off in his car. "Dinner!" Gregory thought.

Determining the coast to be clear, Gregory leaped from the bushes and ran to the dumpster to claim his prize. Digging through the trash, he found several containers of thrown out food. Saying, "This is as low as it gets," he scooped up the food and ran off.

Justice

"The sign said, 'Welcome to Kansas.' When I read that sign, I literally threw up. I can't explain why. Something is going to happen here, I know it. I can feel it in my bones!"

Gregory was accustomed to logging the day, circumstance, and miles in his journal on a daily basis. Today being no exception, and he continued to write:

"July 7th."

"I got two hundred and fifty miles of Missouri dust under my belt. It only took me twenty five days - that has to be some kind of record! I'm really surprised I haven't gotten sick out here though, that's a miracle in itself."

Needing money in a bad way, he set his sights on the town of *Lenape*. Again he tried to use an ATM machine, but he had trouble once more. This time the message flashed, "Account closed!" Gregory was furious, but he continued the trek Westward. "I'm calling James, next chance I get," was the thought that consumed his mind.

He got the chance to make that phone call the following evening, at a place called *Lake Clinton*. A desolate place, near Big Springs, it looked much like a ghost town. He found a pay phone located in the middle of an abandoned campground and Gregory dialed the number.

"Operator. May I help you?"
"I'd like to make a collect call." Gregory replied.
"Your name?"
"Greg."
"One moment please … while I connect you."
"Thank you."
"Hello."
"James?"
"Yes?"
"It's me, Greg."
"Greg? It don't sound like you!"
"I'm at Lake Clinton in Missouri."
"Missouri?" After a brief moment of silence, James closed his eyes and shook his head from side to side. "Oh, Greg, you shouldn't be callin' here."
"Why?"
"The FBI stopped by here a couple weeks ago. They were asking a lot of questions. They say you're a fugitive, Greg. They say you murdered a girl. God, Greg! What have you done?"
James didn't realize it, but two FBI agents were watching his apartment from the street below. Two more agents were listening to their conversation over a phone tap from several blocks away. A federal judge in New York had written the order for the wire tap a week earlier. As he listened in, an agent wrote "Water!" on a card and slid it to his partner. He in turn wrote "West!" on a card and slid it back across the table.
"I didn't do it. I'm being set up." Gregory replied.
"Greg, you got to turn yourself in."
"No, I can't do that right now."

"What are you goin' do?"

"I don't know."

"I got more bad news, Greg."

"Speaking of bad news, why isn't my ATM card working, James?"

"It's all gone."

"What's all gone?"

"The money."

"The money? What are you talking about?"

"I made some bad investments, I lost it all!"

"Oh no … you got to be kidding!"

"I wish … I were."

"So, that's the bad news right?"

"No, there's more."

"There's more?"

"Angela's dead."

"Oh … God … no."

"She overdosed on pills."

There was silence on the other end of the line.

James continued by saying. "L" ran away. They said she didn't want to live with your father-in-law. She's gone, Greg. Nobody knows where she went."

"Is that it, or is there more?"

"No … that's it." After a pause, James said, "Isn't that enough?"

"Yeah … I would think so."

"I'm so sorry! What can I do, man?"

"Nothing, I guess. It will just have to play itself out."

"Be careful!"

"Yeah." Gregory slowly hung the phone up, then rested his forehead against it.

Agent Winn was notified of the suspect's location by the New York field office and he booked the next flight to Wichita.

Traveling around Topeka, Gregory made a stop outside Pauline, then again at Mill Creek beside Alna on his way to *Milford Lake*.

Making camp at Milford Lake, Gregory hid in a cove on a secluded part of the lake. Late afternoon arrived, and Gregory was preparing to pack up his belongings when he heard an outboard motor approaching. Gregory stamped out the fire and hid behind a tree. As the boat drew closer, the fishermen's curiosity got the best of him. Seeing smoke, he drew even closer. Shutting the motor off, the fisherman drifted toward shore. Seeing that someone was there, he yelled. "Who's there?"

Gregory didn't make a sound.

The angler repeated his cry. "Who's there?"

Stepping backwards slightly, Gregory broke a branch lying under foot.

Hearing that, the fishermen repeated himself. This time with more urgency in his voice, he said: "I said! Who's there?"

Thinking his days on the run were over, Gregory walked out from behind the tree with his hands raised.

As he stared at Gregory, the angler began putting two and two together.

"Hey … I know you from somewhere? Where was it?"

Gregory shrugged his shoulders.

"Now I remember! You're that guy I bumped into in Ohio. Lake Madison … Yeah … that's right!"

Realizing that Gregory was a wanted man, the fishermen started his motor up to say, "I don't want any trouble, man! You go your way and I'll go mine, OK?"

As the angler began to drive off, Gregory yelled, "No … you don't understand!"

The fishermen drove away at top speed and Gregory panicked. He quickly packed his belongings and got out of there as fast as he could. The angler drove straight to the Geary County Sheriff's Department to report the incident. The sheriff's office immediately called the FBI in Wichita. Agent Fleming of the Wichita office took the call. He and agent Peters were to be assigned the case. Their supervisor informed them that an agent Winn was on his way from the Indianapolis office.

"I want full cooperation from you two." The supervisor said. "Winn's taking the lead on this one." Staring at the two agents, the supervisor said, "I want this guy. We're close on this one, boys … real close!"

Agents Fleming and Peters nodded their heads in agreement.

Following 18, Gregory would made stops near Vine Creek and Westfall before making his way over to *Lake Wilson*.

Gregory finally reached the banks of *Lake Wilson* under the cover of darkness, and he began to unload his things in preparation for making camp for the day. He had no idea he was being watched, nor did he realize God's hand was in it all.

While using his flashlight, Gregory dropped it. The flashlight hit a rock and made a loud noise. Gregory visually scanned the lake to see if anyone detected the noise; he saw nothing. Gregory illuminated himself by picking the flashlight up, then quickly turned it off, but that didn't go unnoticed.

Sitting in the dark was an off duty sheriff's deputy from Russell County. Deputy Jones would often fish in total darkness - it was his favorite form of relaxation. He loved to sit on the large rocks that bordered the dam; he thought it peaceful. The deputy liked to fish for catfish off the dam at night. With his line on the bottom, he would wrap his finger around the line in anticipation of a bite. Tonight was no exception.

Deputy Jones was almost asleep when he heard Gregory rustle through the weeds. He thought it was odd for anyone to be there so late at night. Watching from a short distance away, the deputy could see and hear everything Gregory was doing. When Gregory dropped his flashlight, Deputy Jones knew this was the man everybody was looking for. He knew the suspect was in the area, and had read the report just a day before. He also familiarized himself with the FBI profile of Gregory, but that backpack stood out like a sore thumb to the deputy.

Crawling quietly through the grass, Deputy Jones made his way over the dam to the spillway below. He used his cell phone to call the Sheriff at home.

"Hello." The Sheriff answered.

"Sir … it's Deputy Jones."

"Ralph, why ya callin' me? Do you know what time it is?"

"Sir, I think we got our man."

"What are you talkin' about?"

"Gregory Matthews is on Lake Wilson!"

"Are you sure?"

"I'm positive, Sir! He matches the description and he's got a backpack."

"Stay put and keep an eye on him. And Ralph…"

"Yes Sir."

"Lay low, don't be a hero!"

"Yes Sir."

Deputy Jones crawled back to the top of the dam and the Sheriff called in the FBI.

Within a few hours it was daylight. Agents Winn, Fleming and Peters arrived on the scene with some of the Sheriff's men. They parked about a mile away then quietly made their way to the top of the dam where Deputy Jones was waiting.

"Sheriff, take your men and block the entrance to this place." Winn said.

"Give us twenty minutes to get in position." The Sheriff replied.

Winn said, "Set your watches men … we go in twenty!"

Twenty minutes later, Winn, Fleming and Peters began to low crawl through the weeds until they were only a few feet away from Gregory. The agents could tell Gregory was asleep, for he was lying on top of his sleeping bag. Winn silently motioned for Peters to follow him in for the capture. Pulling their weapons out, Winn and Peters inched their way over to Gregory. With his weapon drawn, Peters stood beside Winn and aimed at Gregory's head.

Placing the barrel of his 9mm pistol to Gregory's nose, Winn said: "Matthews!"

Gregory woke to the sight of guns staring down at him.

"Are you Gregory Matthews?" Winn said.

Gregory nodded his head.

"You're under arrest for the murder of Katie Lynn Rogers. Peters … cuff him." Winn said.

As Fleming stood guard from a distance, Peters forced Gregory over on his stomach and pried his hands behind his back to handcuff him.

"You have the right to remain silent." Were Winn's instructions to Gregory.

For seemingly no reason at all, Peters stood up, placed his revolver in its holster and kicked Gregory in the ribs as hard as he could. "Not so smart … now are ya punk!" Peters shouted.

"That's enough!" Winn replied. "Anything you say can and will be used against you in a court of law," Winn continued.

Peters kicked Gregory again, saying, "Did ya have fun bashing her head in while you were rapin' her?"

Winn yelled, "I said that's enough!" He paused and then continued. "If you can't afford an attorney you will be given one."

Peters began to repeatedly kick Gregory.

Winn drew his weapon, cocked the hammer back, and placed it behind the ear of Peters. "Stand down Peters … or I'll blow your mind across the lake!" Seeing what was going on, Fleming ran over to Peters and pulled him away from Gregory.

"What is the matter with you?" Fleming asked Peters.

"My girl got raped last year, and they never caught the guy." Peters replied.

"What makes you think this guy raped your daughter?" Fleming asked.

"I don't know if he did or not, it doesn't matter … His type are scum!"

"You do somethin' like that again, I'll shoot ya myself!" Fleming replied.

Winn picked Gregory up from the ground and began walking him to the car when he told Peters and Fleming to: "Take a hike around the lake, both of ya!"

"But!" Peters responded.

"I said, take a hike!" Winn shouted.

Peters and Fleming then walked away.

With his prisoner still handcuffed, Winn held Gregory's head down while opening the door and pushing him into the front seat. Walking around to the driver's side, Winn then got in the car.

Winn said, "Hold your hands out."

"Why?" Gregory replied.

"Just do it." Winn insisted.

Holding his hands out from behind his back, Gregory was released from the cuffs by Winn.

"What's the catch?" Gregory asked.

"We're going to have a little talk, and if you do anything stupid, believe me, I won't hesitate to put a bullet in ya."

"I already did that." Gregory replied.

"Did what?"

"Something stupid."

"The first thing you did that was stupid was run." Winn replied.

"Yeah, you got that right!"

Agent Winn began to question Gregory about the murder in Ohio.

With his hand a rest on his side arm, Winn said, "Start at the beginning and tell me what you saw at the lake that night."

Gregory countered with, "You believe I'm innocent, right?"

"Just start at the beginning … Tell me what you saw."

"Well, I was camping on Lake Madison that night when I heard someone screaming. When I looked over there, well, I saw three boys raping a girl. One was on top and two were holding her down. The girl scratched the guy's face that was on top and he hit her in the head with a rock. When I saw that, I started yelling and I ran over there. The boys jumped in the car and took off. I tried CPR on the girl, but it was too late. I picked her up and walked out of the park, I tried to find help. That's when the Sheriff arrested me. Well … you know the rest. Why, are you asking me all this?"

"You might say the Sheriff's story is full of holes."

"So, what makes you think that?" Gregory replied.

"Well, first of all, why would you be walking down the road with a dead body in your arms. Secondly, I don't believe the Sheriff's nephew when he says a dog scratched his face. And third, I think the Sheriff lies. I think you're being set up, my friend."

Gregory shouted, "Oh, God! Thank you!"

Agent Winn stared at Gregory in silence.

"Now, what?" Gregory then paused before saying. "By the way … what's your name anyway?"

"It's Winn. Agent Larry Winn."

"What makes you think a Jury will believe my story over Sheriff McCants's?"

"They probably won't, that's why the government needs your help."

"My help? Why does the government need my help?" Gregory asked.

"I need your help to lay a trap for Sheriff McCants." Winn replied.

Thinking, Gregory replied, "If it clears my name, just tell me what to do."

"Good, then let's get started!"

Winn honked the horn, and when Peters and Fleming returned to the car all four men drove off.

The agency hid Gregory in room 33 of a motel near Bunker Hill, Kansas. Agent Winn got all the clearances needed to set it up. The FBI, with Gregory's help, spent the next two weeks planning their strategy. It then came time to set the trap and hopefully Sheriff McCants would walk into it.

Nervously dialing the Sheriff's private number, Gregory placed the call. Agents Winn, Fleming and Kline were listening in on the anticipated conversation. Agent Peters had been reassigned to another case a week earlier.

"It's ringing." Gregory quietly whispered to the three.

They were listening through their headsets from only a few feet away.

Looking at Gregory, Winn silently twirled his finger as to say *Let's go*!

"Hello."   The Sheriff answered.

"Sheriff, do you know who this is?"

"No … should I?"

"It's Gregory Matthews."

"How'd you get this number?"

"It's not important." Gregory then paused to say, "I got ya, Sheriff!"

"What are you talking about?"

"I got photos of your nephew killing the girl."

"You're lying." The Sheriff answered with a calm tone.

"Am I?" Gregory replied.

"What'd you do with the camera? I didn't see any camera or film when I busted ya!"

"You must really think I'm stupid." Gregory paused for a moment, then went on to say, "I dropped it in the ditch when you arrested me. I went back and picked it up later. You never saw it, but I must admit … the pictures turned out quite well."

As he began to lose his temper, the Sheriff asked, "What do you want?"

"Well, I was thinking about an extended vacation in Mexico." Raising the tone of his voice, Gregory went on to say, "I want fifty thousand dollars in small unmarked bills … twenties."

"That's gonna take some time to get that together." The Sheriff replied.

"You got till Friday morning."

"How do I know you haven't made more copies?"

"I guess you'll just have to trust me, won't ya?"

As he yelled into the phone, the Sheriff said, "For fifty thousand dollars, I want you to leave the country for good. I want those photos and the negatives too!"

"For fifty grand, you then get a get out of jail free card, Sheriff." Gregory laughed.

"Where do you want the money taken to?" McCants asked.

"Bring it to the Fort Hayes truck stop Friday morning. It's on Interstate 70 in Kansas."

"I know where it's at!" The Sheriff answered in anger.

"Be there at seven in the morning. If you're not there by 7:30, the deal's off. And Sheriff." Gregory paused.

"What?"

"Don't do anything stupid … or I'll blow the whistle."

"I'll be there." The Sheriff said before hanging up.

McCants had no intention of paying Gregory the money or seeing him live.

Friday morning came and the Sheriff arrived right on time. Sheriff McCants walked through the front door of the truck stop at 7:02. Wearing civilian clothing, McCants carried a bag. He walked over to where Gregory was sitting and sat down. The Sheriff never realized it to be a setup. FBI agents blocked the entrance road to the truck stop shortly after the Sheriff walked in. There were also agents stationed outside in parked vehicles.

Looking across the table at the Sheriff, Gregory asked, "You got the money?"

"Yeah." The Sheriff answered.

"Let's see it!" Gregory said.

"Let's see the photos first." McCants countered.

The Sheriff couldn't allow Gregory to look inside the bag; it was full of cut up newspapers.

McCants was angry and didn't notice that he and Gregory were the only customers in there. The waitress walked over to the table and said, "May I take your order?"

She was really FBI agent Sims, a veteran of the agency for the past fifteen years. The busboy, cook and manager were also FBI agents.

The Sheriff said, "Bring us a couple of coffees."

After the waitress left, Sheriff McCants pulled a gun from his pocket and cocked it. Pointing it at Gregory under the table, he said, "The game's over Matthews!"

Talking in a raised tone of voice, Gregory said, "What are you going to do, Sheriff, shoot me?"

Sheriff McCants never thought to check Gregory for a wire. Taped to his chest, was a microphone under his clothes. Their conversation was being recorded. An agent in the back room of the truck stop was listening to every word.

That agent then broadcast the word *Gun* to all who were listening. The only agents inside who didn't have a listening device in their ears were Sims and the Cook. The agent in the back room then wrote the word *Gun* on a piece of paper, exited the back room, and handed it to Sims and the Cook while the Sheriff wasn't looking.

Stalling, as he tried to get a taped confession out of the Sheriff, Gregory said, "So … tell me why you're covering up the murder, Sheriff?"

"Because I can't stand your type!"

"Oh … what type might that be, Sheriff?"

"Religious freaks, that's what! My worthless old man was one." McCants said in an angry tone.

"So you admit your nephew killed her?"

"Yeah … but you'll never live to talk about it. Now get up!"

Gregory stood and so did the Sheriff. With a gun pointed in Gregory's back, the McCants said, "Start walkin'!"

Seeing the gun and what was going on, agent Sims signaled the Cook. He yelled "Order up" while standing over a microphone that was mounted over the grill. "Order up" was the code word for *Let's move in*. As they took their positions, several agents lay in wait outside.

As soon as Gregory and McCants stepped out the door, an undercover agent bumped into the Sheriff. That agent was a decoy. Dressed in a cowboy hat and boots, he pretended to be a customer who was entering the truck stop. His job was to distract the Sheriff, and it worked.

McCants momentarily lost his concentration. Turning his attention to the cowboy and away from Gregory, he said, "Watch where you're goin'!"

The agent said, "Screw you, pal!"

McCants then turned the gun on the agent. Seeing that, the agent grabbed the Sheriff's arm holding the gun and forced it into the air as McCants fired three rounds. Gregory ran for cover when he saw the struggle break out. McCants tried to aim at Gregory, but missed while firing twice more. Three more agents, including Winn, rushed in to wrestle McCants to the ground. One of the agents was accidentally shot in the leg by McCants when they tried to apprehend him. He would fully recover from the wound later.

As agent Winn was handcuffing McCants, he said, "You're under arrest for conspiracy, attempted murder and whatever else I can think of."

Winn read the Sheriff his rights and sat him in the back seat of a squad car. It was forever etched upon Gregory's mind when he watched the Sheriff being hauled away. McCants stared out the back window of the car at Gregory as it drove off.

Walking up to Gregory, Agent Sims placed a one hundred dollar bill in his hand.

"What's this for?" Gregory asked.

"I'm tipping you." Sims said. As she was walking away, the agent said, "There's nothing worse than a crooked cop."

Winn soon walked over to Gregory to extend his hand. "You're free to go!" He said.

As he shook the agent's hand, Gregory said, "What do you need to be set freed from … Agent Winn?"

Trying hard to hold it all back Agent Winn asked, "Can I buy you a cup of coffee?"

Both men entered the truck stop and sat down. Agent Winn went on to tell Gregory his story of salvation, one that no one else knew of. Agent Larry Winn was a man who believed in second chances, he himself being given one.

Winn told Gregory he shot a 13-year-old boy by accident one night while on patrol. Being new to law enforcement, he was suspended and put under investigation. While standing in a dark alley one night, Winn almost took his own life. He placed a gun in his mouth and cocked it. Feeling a tap on his shoulder, Winn removed the gun from his mouth and turned around to aim it. Standing there, with his hands above his head, was Brother Tom, a street preacher. Brother Tom led Winn to the Lord that night, and the agent's life would never be the same. The charges were eventually dropped along with the investigation. Winn was reinstated, but with regret he never saw Brother Tom again.

Gregory left Fort Hayes with a renewed sense of hope. He wrote about stops made in Voda, Grainfield, Mingo, Edson, and Goodland, but none of them were as noteworthy as Fort Hayes.

Before stepping over into Colorado, Gregory wrote:

"It's September 7th, a day to remember! I was a fugitive in Kansas for two months, but I leave here a free man. Kansas was a big state, over five hundred miles of trouble, but now - FREEDOM! After five states of being on the run, I'm truly free!"

Gregory decided to travel by day once again, starting tomorrow.

As he jumped up and down, while dancing in the moonlight, Gregory shouted, "Free at last, free at last, thank God almighty, I'm free at last!"

A New Dawn

Gregory awoke in the morning to a new outlook on life. Filled with a new sense of purpose, he packed his bag for the day ahead. Before leaving, he fell to his knees, bowed his head, and interlocked his fingers.

"Lord, it's the dawn of a new day, I thank you for that. I made you a promise back there. I said if you got me out of that mess I would serve you the rest of my life. You kept your end of the bargain, now I'm keeping mine. I'm forever grateful, thanks for sparing me from that. I'll go wherever you tell me to go and do whatever you tell me to do. Oh, before I forget, I forgive Sheriff McCants and his nephew for what they've done. Lord, shine your light upon them, that they may come to know you. Continue to keep your hand upon Katie Lynn Rogers's parents, Lord. Give em' peace, give em' peace. Amen."

It was getting late in the afternoon, and Gregory wasn't far from *Bethune*. He saw a set of railroad tracks that stretched across a river and through a trestle bridge. Always being fascinated by engineering and architecture, Gregory couldn't resist checking it out.

Stepping onto the bridge, Gregory thought, "This thing's a modern marvel!" He loved the program with that title, it being his favorite show. Looking down, he could see the river below through the track supports. A long one, Gregory decided to cross it after all. Walking at a safe pace, Gregory could hear a train coming in the distance. Thinking he had plenty of time, he didn't hurry. About halfway across, he turned to see the train coming. With a sense of urgency to his step, he began to run. Only a few feet from the end, Gregory thought, "I'm gonna make it," but then he tripped and fell. As it slid off his shoulder, Gregory lost his grip on the backpack. It bounced once then fell over the side to plunge in the river below. Shaken and cut, Gregory crawled to the end of the bridge and quickly rolled out of the way, the train just barely missing him. Watching his backpack float downstream, Gregory groaned, "Great!"

After quite some time, Gregory got to his feet. Not knowing what he would do without his belongings, he brushed himself off. Thinking to himself, "It's always something," and he would never see that backpack again, he continued on. Downstream, another one of God's miraculous plans was about to unfold. You might say the Creator was once again being himself, the great, *"I Am."*

Not far upstream from the bridge, a father and his son were motoring with the current in their boat when they saw Gregory fall. The father told his son, "I hope he's alright," as they continued on their way to their favorite fishing hole.

Traveling under the bridge and several yards past, the father saw something floating on the water. He yelled, "Son, I'll swing by and you grab it out of the water, ok?" The boy nodded. Pulling the backpack into the boat, the father decided to run the boat to shore and check its contents.

On shore, the father discovered Gregory's belongings and his personal journal. Looking at his son, the father had an astonished look on his face.

"What's wrong, Daddy?"

"There's nothing wrong, Billy. I'm just amazed that none of this stuff inside here is wet. The outside of the bag doesn't even look damp either. Why didn't it sink?" After rolling the thought around in his mind for a while, the father looked at his son. "Son, I know I promised you a day of fishing, but we must do something more important."

"What is it Daddy?"

"Well, remember what they been teachin' you in Sunday school?"

"Yes, Daddy … To be honest."

"Billy, Daddy wasn't going to be honest today. He was going to keep that guy's stuff. That's wrong. What do ya say we try to catch that trout another day."

"What do you mean, Daddy?"

"Let's me and you park the boat under the bridge and track that guy down so we can give him back his stuff."

"That would be a good thing to do, wouldn't it, Daddy?"

"Yes, son, it would."

Billy hugged his dad and said, "I'm proud of you Daddy!"

A tear began to roll down the father's cheek.

An hour or two later, the father and son caught up with Gregory. Sitting on a rock, Gregory was in thought of what to do when the father and son approached. Holding the backpack to his side, the father said, "Stranger, I think we have something that belongs to you."

"Oh God, thank you." Gregory replied.

Extending his hand, the father said, "I'm Jim."

After shaking hands with Gregory, the father placed his hand on his son's head and said, "And this here is my son, Billy."

Bending down to look Billy in the face, Gregory said, "Glad to meet you, Billy. My name's Gregory, but my friends call me Greg."

With a shy look, Billy turned to the side to say, "Hi."

Before deciding to leave, Jim and Billy offered to help Gregory make camp.   After they finished making camp, Billy made a suggestion.

"Daddy, can we camp out with our friend tonight?"

Turning to his son, Jim said, "I don't know, son."

"The angel said it was ok, Daddy."

Looking to Gregory, Jim had a puzzled look on his face. Turning back to his son, Jim said, "What?"

"I was praying last night in my room when an angel came in."

Looking to Gregory, Jim said, "Six year olds sure do have a sense of imagination."

"No, Daddy, it's true."

"Now stop it." Jim told his son.

Gregory looked over at Jim and said, "Let him talk."

Chuckling, Jim said, "Ok son … go ahead."

Billy went on to say, "I was praying in my room last night when an angel stopped by. She said that me and you were going to meet a stranger today, Daddy. She said he was a minister. He's on a trip to wash his soul, Daddy. She told me to tell him that God loves him."

Getting angry, Jim said, "Stop it Billy, that's enough!"

Turning to Gregory to apologize for his son's behavior, Jim noticed that Gregory was crying.

"I'm sorry." Jim said.

Looking to Jim, Gregory said, "It's true. Everything your son said … is true."

"I find that hard to believe." Jim said.

"It's all true. I'm called to preach and I'm on a journey to cleanse my soul. I'm headed for Los Angeles."

"I still find it hard to believe." Jim replied.

"How do you explain the bag not getting wet." Gregory asked.

"I can't." Jim answered.

After a few moments of silence, Jim asked his son, "Are you sure that's what you want to do? Spend the night out here?"

Billy nodded his head up and down many times as to say, "Yes."

"I'll call Mom on the cell phone and tell her what we're doing." Jim told his son.

Jim's wife thought the idea was crazy, but in the end gave it her blessing. Billy, Jim, and Gregory spent most of the night talking about Gregory's adventures. Very early the next morning, Jim walked back to the boat and gathered up their

supplies and made his way back to camp. Before
Gregory woke, Jim picked up his son, who was still
asleep, and placed him on his shoulder. Without
waking Gregory, Jim made his way back to the boat
and eventually home. Gregory woke up a short time
later to food, clothes, and money that was lying on
the ground in front of him. Jim left without saying
goodbye, but in his own way he did.

 After making brief stops in Flagler and Agate,
Gregory stumbled upon *Cherry Creek Lake* just
outside Denver.

 On an extended leave of absence from the paper,
the editor of the Columbus Dispatch was
visiting a friend. His friend was the owner of the
Denver Post newspaper; he also owned the Maria
on Cherry Creek Lake. Driving to the lake for a day
of pleasure were the owner and his friend the editor.
While crossing the bridge, the editor noticed a man
standing on the bridge that overlooked the lake.
Traveling several feet before realizing who it was,
the editor yelled at his friend to stop.

 "Back up, Fred!" The editor shouted.

 "What for?" The driver replied.

 "Just do it!"

Backing up on the bridge, the truck came to a
stop beside Gregory. The editor rolled down the
passenger window to speak with Gregory.

 "Are you Gregory Matthews?" The editor asked.

 "Yes, why?"

 "I'm Jerry Rogers!"

 With a blank look on his face, Gregory said,
"Do I know you?"

 "I'm Katie Lynn Rogers's uncle."

Throwing his hands up in the air, Gregory said, "I don't want any trouble."

"I'm not here for that."

"Then what is it you want." Gregory asked.

"Can we talk?"

"I guess so," was Gregory's reply.

"There's a restaurant just over the hill. Jump in, I'll buy ya a cup of coffee."

"I'll meet ya there." Gregory replied as he started to walk.

Gregory met the two men at the restaurant and he sat down at their table.

After ordering, Jerry said, "I've come a long way to meet you Mr. Matthews. I've been trying to find you for weeks, so I could thank you. It's quite a stroke of luck that we meet like this, don't you think?"

"I don't believe in luck." Gregory replied.   He went on to say, "So, what do you have on your mind?"

"I was really close to Katie, and unfortunately, our paper was the first to do the story of her murder. When I heard the news … well … I lost it!" Staring at Gregory, Jerry said, "I wanted to kill you Matthews! Then one day my secretary threw the AP story from Wichita on my desk. The one where you brought the man back from death at the flea market."

Gregory interrupted to say, "I didn't do that … God did."

Jerry went on, "Then I read the story of the Sheriff's arrest along with his nephew and friends from the Topeka press release." Looking down,

Jerry said, "I was wrong about you, Matthews. I came out here to thank you for what you did. You risked your life so the real killer could be found. Our family appreciates that."

"You're welcome Mr. Rogers." Gregory replied.

"Matthews, my friend and I are newspaper men and we would like to ask a favor of you."

"What is it?" Gregory replied.

"My friend owns a publishing company. We're thinkin' about publishing your book."

"What book?" Gregory asked.

"*Moses, the true story of a modern day hero with a backpack*."

"What are you talking about?"

"I want the rights to write your biography, Matthews. My friend here promises to publish it."

"I'm not interested." Gregory replied.

"Why not?"

"I'm just not. I'm curious though, how'd you come up with that title?"

"That's what they've been calling you Matthews. Moses!"

Laughing, Gregory said, "Who?"

"That's what the papers have been calling you, a Modern-Day Moses."

"Really?"

Jerry stood to extend his hand to Gregory. "Well, Matthews, I guess this is goodbye then. If you change your mind, here's my card." As he handrd his business card to Gregory, Jerry said, "You can't stop me from writing a feature story in my paper though. It'll be one of good that triumphs over evil, Matthews."

While shaking the editor's hand, Gregory nodded his head and said, "I'm glad you found closure to all this Mr. Rogers."

Continuing to travel Westward, Gregory set his sights on the peak of Mt. Evans. With a prior stop made in Mornson, Gregory made his way up the 14,260' ascent. Along the way, he would experience God's amazing grace once more at a place called *Echo Lake*.

As he walked by it, Gregory thought, there's a lot of activity on that lake for a Sunday morning. A large banner hanging over the entrance said, "Welcome anglers! Bassmaster hosts the Echo Lake Grand." Gregory noticed quite a few big rigs parked there, they appeared to be corporate sponsors. Something else caught Gregory's attention. He could hear shouts coming from a tent down near the lake. Wanting to see what all the excitement was, Gregory ventured down towards the tent.

Gregory walked inside the tent, removed his backpack, and took a seat in the back. There were only a handful of people in there, but they sure were a rowdy bunch. Gregory couldn't believe what he was seeing. Jimmy Thornton, his favorite professional bass pro, was conducting a Sunday morning service for all the other anglers. Jimmy gave a stirring sermon. Many were raising their hands and shouting.

At the conclusion of his sermon, Jimmy looked to the back and stared at Gregory.

Pointing at Gregory, Jimmy said, "You're that gentleman they've been talking about on the radio, aren't you?"

Gregory looked back at Jimmy with a blank stare.

"You're that guy they call Moses, aren't you?"

Gregory shook his head while thinking to himself, "Please don't embarrass me."

"Come up here, son!" Jimmy said.

Reluctantly, Gregory walked to the front.

Holding the microphone to his side and extending his hand, Jimmy said, "I'm Jimmy."

Shaking his hand, Gregory said, "I know who you are Mr. Thornton. I'm Gregory Matthews, your biggest fan."

"Lead us in a prayer, would you?" Jimmy asked.

Gregory said, "I'd be glad to."

Holding the microphone back to his mouth, Jimmy announced that Gregory would be leading them in a prayer.

As he held the mike, Gregory said, "Father, we come before you today with a humble heart. Although fishing is a way of life to these men, show them what's really important to you. Make them fishers of men, Lord. In Jesus's holy name … I pray. Amen."

Everyone in attendance stood to applaud, including Jimmy. As they filed out, Jimmy gave Gregory the opportunity of a lifetime.

"Gregory, Bassmaster gives out one invitation to amateur anglers at each stop on the tour. I'm the acting chairman for today and I'd like to give you that invite, my friend."

"I appreciate that, but I don't have a boat or tackle." Gregory replied.

After much thought, Jimmy said, "Well … just consider it a kind gesture then, one that can be framed on the wall."

"Will you autograph it for me?" Gregory asked.

After signing it to say, "Good luck my friend," Jimmy Thornton left.

A short while later, Gregory was down near the lake skipping rocks across the water. An old man walked up to Gregory to ask, "You're the man they call Moses, aren't you?"

"I don't care for the name, but yes, that's what they call me." Gregory replied.

Extending his hand, the old man said, "I'm Enoch."

Gregory offered to shake the old man's hand by holding out his. Enoch placed a folded five hundred dollar bill in Gregory's hand. Looking at the bill, Gregory said, "What's this?"

"It's the tournament entrance fee. Take the money and your invitation over to the sign-in booth. You don't have much time left."

As he looked at the old man, Gregory said, "Thanks for the thought, but I don't have any equipment."

Pointing at an old row boat, that Gregory never noticed before, the old man said, "Use my boat. You'll find a can of worms and a cane pole under it."

Bending down to pick up a rock, Gregory turned to throw it in the lake. After he skipped it across the water he turned around to say "No Thanks" to the kind stranger, but Enoch was nowhere to be found.

A cold chill ran up Gregory's spine, making the hair on his neck stand up.

Once he used his invitation and paid the entrance fee, Gregory walked over to the boat. "That's a really old boat," Gregory thought. When he slipped it over, there was a long cane pole and a can of worms under there just like Enoch said it would be. It being the last day of the tournament, Gregory thought, "There's no way I can win this thing!" He pushed the boat into the water and began to fish only a few yards from shore.

When he went through the sign-in process the tournament director told Gregory the competition would end at four o'clock. He also said that when the horn blew at the end of the day, all anglers were to weigh-in their fish.

It was late in the day and something told Gregory to cast his bait on the other side of the boat. He immediately hooked a seven pound largemouth bass. He then landed a five pounder and then a ten pounder before the horn sounded.

Back at the weigh-in station, the competition boiled down to Gregory and Jimmy Thornton. Jimmy also had a combined total of three fish for the tournament, but his fish weighed three ounces less than Gregory's.

Jimmy handed Gregory a check for ten thousand dollars, then said, "Stay with us. Tour the circuit with me."

As he tried to hold back the tears, Gregory replied, "I didn't come this far to quit the journey, Jimmy. I'm in some what of a tournament myself, a tournament for souls."

As Jimmy shook Gregory's hand, he said, "I appreciate that, my friend."

Gregory wanted to thank Enoch before he left Echo Lake that day, but no one there knew him. Not a single soul had ever heard of an old man named Enoch who owned a row boat. When Gregory walked back to where he left the boat it was gone. As he stood there staring, wondering what he had witnessed, that same cold chill ran through him again.

Gregory traveled down the other side of the mountain the following day and stopped at the town of Keystone. He went to the Keystone National Bank that afternoon and handed that prize money check to a teller, to say, "I'd like to cash that."

As the teller looked at the check, she asked, "Do you have an account with us, sir?"

Gregory's reply was, "No."

"There will be a five dollar fee and I will have to see some identification." The teller responded.

Gregory handed his ID to the teller and waited as she examined it.

"I will have to have my supervisor take a look at this, sir."

With her supervisor's attention gained, the teller called him over.

"Mr. Flint, I got this check for ten thousand dollars that the gentleman wants to cash. He doesn't have an account with us. What do you want me to do?"

Mr. Flint noticed that it was a Bassmaster check. He once more asked for Gregory's ID and he examined it.

As he looked up at Gregory, the supervisor said, "You're that Moses guy I read about in the paper. You won that tournament at Echo Lake. You beat Jimmy Thornton … man!" With the shake of his head, Flint said, "That was unbelievable!"

Gregory smiled to say nothing, just hoping he would cash the check.

"How would you like this Mr. Matthews? In large … or small bills?"

"Hundreds would be fine." Gregory replied.

As Mr. Flint was snaking Gregory's hand, the teller began to count out the money. No longer hurting for cash, Gregory spent that evening in a nearby campground.

A couple of evenings later, Gregory walked into the *Redcliff* campground and into the lives of Wilbur Sutton and his wife Mary. As the campground's office door closed behind Gregory, the bell mounted on the top of the door rang. Sitting on a stool behind the counter, reading the paper, was an elderly man who had a smile as big as the state of Colorado.

"Are you the owner?" Gregory asked.

As Gregory extended his hand, the man extended his, but he kept staring at Gregory with a puzzled look. Looking down at the paper, while shaking Gregory's hand, he said, "I'm Wilbur Sutton, Mr. Matthews, I own this place."

Surprised, Gregory asked, "How do you know my name?"

Folding the paper over, and sliding it to Gregory, Wilbur said, "You're front page news. The

Denver television stations ran your story last night, too!"

Looking at the paper, then pushing it to the side, Gregory said, "I would just like a good night's sleep, Mr. Sutton."

Pulling out his money, Gregory asked, "How much do I owe you for one night in a primitive spot?"

Wilbur answered with, "Your money's no good here!"

Thinking Wilbur developed a bad impression of him; Gregory started to walk towards the door.

Yelling to the backroom, Wilbur said, "Mother, we got Moses in camp!"

Stepping out from behind the counter, Wilbur pushed Gregory's hand away from the door knob and closed the door. Not knowing what to make of it all, Gregory stood back. Then Wilbur's wife entered the room.

Wilbur said, "Mother, this is Gregory Matthews … Moses. Mr. Matthews, this is my wife, Mary."

Gregory shook hands with the woman, then said, "Maam, your husband's blocking the door."

After reaching into his pocket Wilbur threw Gregory a set of keys. Catching the keys, Gregory said, "What are these for?"

"They're for our new RV out back." Mary replied.

"Stay in it as long as you like." Wilbur added.

Trying to hold back the tears of a questioning heart, Gregory asked, "Why are you doing this?"

Mary told Gregory she had a dream the night before. In her dream, she said a young man entered their office. The Lord told Mary, in the dream, she would recognize him.   She went on to explain that while standing in the office, a bright beam of light surrounded the man. The Lord concluded the dream by saying, "His name will be watchman." Mary said she was instructed to bless the man who will bless so many more.

After Mary finished talking, Gregory asked, "So, you and your husband are Christians?"

"For many years" she replied.

Gregory spent several days with the Suttons, and in the end, became good friends with them.

The next two stops were also in campgrounds, Eagle and Glenwood Springs. The owners of those sites were also generous. They wouldn't accept any money, but provided the best accommodations in camp. Gregory never knew the reason why they did that, until shortly before he left Glenwood Springs. With beautiful Bald Mountain in the background, Gregory reluctantly started to pack his belongings. The owner of the campsite noticed Gregory was leaving and walked over to him. He said, "Son, you have wonderful friends in Wilbur and Mary Sutton."

"Why do you say that?" Gregory countered.

"You know why!" The owner replied.

"Am I missing something here?" Gregory snapped back.

"You ungrateful jerk!" The owner shouted.

"What are you talking about?" Gregory asked.

In an angry tone, the owner said, "You're just using them … aren't you?"

"I have no idea what you're talking about."

"Wilbur and Mary are my friends and I don't like what you're trying to pull."

As Gregory shook his head, he said, "I really don't understand what you're talking about."

"Who do you think paid for your stay? Who do you think called all the campgrounds West of here and said bill me for it. Who do you think said bless him with the best?"

Shaking his head once more, Gregory said, "I didn't know!"

The owner said, "Well … now you know!" Then he walked away, still quite upset.

Gregory went on to make a brief stop in Parachute before making camp outside *Grand Junction*, but he never forgot the kindness of the Suttons.

Warming himself by the fire, Gregory was surprised to see a limousine park on the side of the road only a few yards away. He saw a man dressed in blue jeans and a T-shirt get out of the back, then motion the driver on as he stepped away from the vehicle. The man walked up to Gregory, then introduced himself.

"I'm Doug Love, Mayor of Grand Junction."

As he shook the Mayor's hand, Gregory said, "What brings you out here, Mr. Mayor."

"Can I share the fire with you?" The Mayor asked.

Extending forth an open hand, Gregory motioned in silence as to say, help yourself.

"So, what brings you out here?" Gregory asked.

"Well, a good friend of mine lives right down the road. You're camping on his property."

Gregory interrupted to say, "I'm sorry, I guess I just wasn't thinking. I'll pack my stuff up right now."

"No, don't worry about that," continuing his conversation, the Mayor said, "My friend was going to call the police, but he thought better of it when he recognized who you were, so he called me. He told me to come see you, ask for prayer. He's a good man … he knows what my family has been going through."

"What's wrong?" Gregory asked.

"My fourteen-year-old daughter has cancer. She doesn't have much time left. We've taken her to the best doctors and the most advanced hospitals, but there's nothing they can do."

Gregory looked at Doug to say, "I know the master physician."

"What's his name?" The Mayor asked excitedly. "Where's he located at?"

"His name is Jesus," said Gregory, "and He's with us tonight."

Doug started to weep. He told Gregory he had promised his mother he would serve the Lord, it was her dying wish. She passed away and he never kept the promise.

Deciding it was time to keep that promise, Doug said a prayer of salvation. Before leading Doug in that prayer, Gregory told him if he truly believed in his heart that all things are possible through Christ, change would come.

Asking if he could spend the night with Gregory, Doug said, "I told the driver to pick me up in the morning. Do you mind, it's a long walk home."

Gregory didn't mind, he enjoyed this new found friendship. While both men lay on their backs, about to go to sleep, several thoughts raced through Gregory's mind. Telling the Mayor of the thoughts, Gregory said, "This may sound off the wall, but your daughter will be completely healed. Your wife's name is Renee, isn't it?"

"Why … yes … it is. How did you know that?"

"I don't know these things, Mr. Mayor … it comes from the Holy Spirit."

Doug became all the more alert.

"The cancer will leave her body three days after the goldfish dies and your wife stops playing the piano." Gregory added.

The Mayor didn't know what to make of that silly little prophesy so he rolled over, said goodnight, and fell asleep.

Early the next morning, the driver picked Doug up and the two men said their good-byes. Doug told his wife about the experience and of what Gregory said, but she didn't believe any of it. All that was about to change though.

About a week after Doug returned from seeing Gregory, Renee placed a vase full of water on top of the piano. The vase contained their daughter's pet goldfish. Sometime during the night, the goldfish jumped out of the vase and landed in the piano, where it died. When Renee discovered what happened, she told her husband she would sell the piano and never play it again if God healed her baby. You see, Renee loved to play the piano and she was quite good at it, but she was willing to sacrifice all that if God spared the life of her girl.

The Love family experienced a miracle that week. Hannah Love, their beautiful fourteen-year-old daughter, miraculously recovered three days after the death of her pet. Her hair grew back soon after and the doctors were puzzled. Renee kept her promise of never playing the piano again and Hannah promised God she would spend the rest of her life telling mankind of His grace and mercy.

Before entering into Utah, Gregory sat on a stump to write the following in his journal:

"September 1st."

"I met lots of wonderful people in Colorado. It's Labor Day and I just put another five hundred miles behind me. They call it the *Beehive State,* but I call Utah the beauty of God's creative hand."

The Following

As he continued to follow the Interstate 70 corridor, cutting through the mountains, Gregory was about five miles south of *Cisco* when he heard children at play. They were swimming at one of the local attractions. During the evolution of the river, a bend formed in the Colorado that cut into the side of a cliff, that landscape masterpiece was called "Big Ben." Jumping from the rocks above to the water below, the kids seemed to be having a lot of fun.

Gregory watched the youngsters for a while; then he turned to walk away. He didn't get far before he heard screams. One of the boys, who couldn't swim, slipped on the wet rocks and fell in the river. Struggling to keep his head above water, the boy finally went under the surface. His friends screamed for help. Gregory threw off his backpack, ran to the edge of the cliff, and dove in.

Gregory grabbed the boy and swam with him to shore. Scared, but okay, the boy thanked Gregory for his kind deed. Gregory told the kids they should be more careful next time and that their parents were probably worried about them. "That's enough swimmin' for today," the boy told his friends.

Gregory made camp there that night. He thought if he stayed there the kids would not come back to get in any more trouble. His idea must have worked because Gregory was the only one who enjoyed watching the stars from "Big Ben" that evening.

Gregory got up the next morning and made himself a nice breakfast. After he finished eating, he packed up his things and got back out on the road. He thought to himself, "If I make good time, I can hit *Crescent Junction* before nightfall." Gregory made good time that day, and he reached the city limits of Crescent Junction just before dark.

Gregory was walking on Route 6, thinking about a nice hotel room, when a van pulled in behind him and parked on the side of the road. A man jumped out of the van and ran towards Gregory. Not knowing what he was doing, Gregory braced for the worst. Out of breath, the man said, "You're the guy who saved my boy at Big Ben yesterday, aren't you?"

Gregory looked over the man's shoulder to see the boy he pulled from the water the day before sitting in the passenger seat, waving at Gregory. Nodding his head while extending his hand, Gregory said, "I'm Gregory Matthews."

"Chuck Springer. Glad to meet you." The father replied.

Pulling his checkbook from his jacket, Chuck started to fill out a check. He wrote the date, Gregory's name, and signed it. On the memo he wrote, "Thanks for saving my boy's life!"

"What are you doing?" Gregory asked.

"I appreciate you saving my boy's life." Handing the check to Gregory, Chuck said, "Fill in the amount."

Gregory's mind said, "Take it," but his heart said, "Don't." He couldn't shake the feeling of "No." Handing the check back to Chuck, Gregory said, "I can't."

Looking at the check, Chuck said, "I don't understand."

"God's telling me don't take it." Was Gregory's reply. "He said, you're gonna need it."

With a really puzzled look on his face, Chuck shook Gregory's hand and walked back to the van. As Chuck started the engine, he pointed at Gregory and told his son, "That guy's crazy!" Was Gregory really crazy? Chuck didn't think so a month later, when he lost his job.

Word spread fast in Eastern Utah of Gregory's heroics. A line of cars slowly formed behind him as he approached the entrance to the Green River State Park. A large majority of the drivers were teenagers who painted things on their vehicles like "Hero," "We love you," and "Thanks." One at a time, each vehicle in the caravan pulled along side Gregory. The occupants would either give him a wave of the hand or a thumbs up. Some yelled or cheered, while others handed him money.   Surprised and overcome by joy, Gregory thought, "I guess I've got a following."

A couple days later, just before lunch, Gregory was walking up the hill towards *San Rafael Knob*. A large passenger van, full of school children, pulled in behind Gregory. A young lady rolled down the driver's window to yell, "Mr. Matthews!"

The woman obviously knows my name, he thought. Gregory's curiosity got the best of him, and he decided to see what she wanted.

As he walked up to the window, Gregory asked, "Can I help you?"

Gregory noticed a not so normal vanload of kids. They didn't yell, scream, or throw things. To the contrary, they were quiet, attentive, and polite.

Glancing at the students then looking at the teacher, Gregory said, "I can tell you rule the classroom with an ironclad fist."

"We have an understanding." the teacher replied. "My name's Wendy Shore."

Gregory began to chuckle when giggles emanated from the back of the vehicle.

"What's so funny, Mr. Matthews?" She inquired.

Trying to wipe the smile from his face, Gregory explained, "I'm sorry, it just sounds like a funny name."

With a stern look on her face, Wendy said, "I get that all the time!"

"What are you doing out here with a van full of kids?" Gregory asked.

"Well, my sixth grade class here begged me for a fieldtrip. Although it wasn't easy, I got permission to use the school's van and here we are. These kids would like to walk with you this afternoon and experience what you're experiencing. Who knows, they may even have a question or two for you. So, what do you think, Mr. Matthews?"

Not giving it much thought that all, Gregory said, "Sure, why not!"

Spending the afternoon with Gregory, the kids had several interesting questions. They seemed to enjoy themselves until Ms. Shore blew her whistle. That meant the fieldtrip was over and it was time to head home. Before leaving, each student thanked Gregory as did Ms. Shore.

Over the horizon the summit lay on the following day, all 7,923' worth of it. Gregory made it to the top of the mountain, but something unusual was happening. As he crested the peak, he became quite frightened by what he saw. In the valley below, storm clouds were developing. As he watched, the front gave birth to a tornado, but it didn't act like a normal twister. The tornado ran up the side of the mountain. Seeing that, Gregory ran for cover. Watching the violent wind race, Gregory noticed something peculiar about it. It was following him, but getting smaller. Only a few feet away, the tornado reduced in size, lifted off the ground, and became a swirl of fire. Captivated, Gregory could only watch as God's glory spun over him, then suddenly it was gone. Gregory later wrote about the experience in his journal. He made remarks about the continual amazement he had for the manifestation of God's power.

Down the other side of the mountain lay *Salina*. His eyes were focused on that community, but four ladies were about to change the vision.

Walking along the outskirts of the town, Gregory noticed the approach of a rather slow moving pick-up. Stopping in the middle of the road, the driver rolled down the window of the vintage Chevrolet. Inside were four elderly women

who were talking among themselves. Not wanting
to give directions, Gregory continued to walk away
from them. Yelling, "Hey, Sonny!" The driver
caught Gregory's attention.

"I'm not from around here." Gregory replied.

"We know that!" She laughed.

"What is it you ladies want?"

Scolded by the others, one of the ladies jokingly
said, "You!"

Gregory just smiled.

The Driver said, "We're from the Salina
Catholic Church." Pointing to her friends, she said:
"This is part of the ladies group. We heard how you
saved that boy's life and we'd like to repay the
kindness."

"I appreciate that ladies, but it's not really
necessary."

Continuing with her explanation, the Driver
said, "We've got some food for you. A young man
like you can't travel on an empty stomach, now can
he?"

"That's nice, ladies, thank you."

"It's in the back, help yourself." The Driver
replied.

Looking in the back of the truck, Gregory
couldn't believe his eyes. The entire bed of the
vehicle was full of groceries.

"Ladies, I can't eat all that!"

One of the passengers said, "He sure does look
skinny to me, girls!"

"Ladies, I've got an idea," Gregory said. "Why
don't I take a few items and you feed the rest to the
homeless. What do ya say?"

The Driver once again shouted, "Help yourself."

After Gregory loaded his backpack with some of the items, he thanked the generous strangers. As they drove off in a cloud of dust, he thought that was the last he'd see of them. He never stopped to realize those ladies had a mission. It wouldn't be his last encounter with those gals.

Passing Salina by, Gregory walked till late afternoon. He was only a mile or two from *White Pine Park* when he started noticing the signs along the road. Every few hundred yards, Gregory saw a sign that said, "Gregory Matthews, come join us!" He followed them into the park as they led to the picnic area.

Walking into the picnic area, Gregory couldn't believe what he saw. Sitting at several of the tables were homeless people. Women were serving them food as they ate. Gregory recognized four of the servers as the ladies from Salina. One of the ladies saw Gregory and walked over to him.

"Glad you could join us, Mr. Matthews. I take it you saw our signs?"

"What's going on here?" Gregory asked.

"Well, me and the girls took your advice. We called our friends, then we went knockin' on some doors. We went to the homeless shelters in the area and told them we were having a picnic. We picked up the less fortunate ones then drove out here for the feast. So, what do ya think of our idea?"

Having a heart for the homeless, Gregory couldn't control his emotions, he broke down and began to weep. Many of the women saw his tears of joy and walked over to him. Many couldn't hug him without crying themselves. Even some of the homeless got in on the act, they just couldn't pass up a group hug. Spending the afternoon there, Gregory enjoyed it beyond measure.

Quite a few days later, Gregory came into sight of Interstate 15 and the watchful eye of the Native American Indians that lived there. As he passed through the *Kanosh Reservation*, Gregory couldn't shake the feeling he was being watched. He felt it at Fishlake, Adamsville, and then again at Little Salt Lake.

As Gregory relaxed in front of the fire that evening, he noticed an eagle in the treetops only yards away as he lay on his back to enjoy the warmth of the flame. He was becoming quite sleepy. As soon as he closed his eyes, he felt the cold blade of a knife at his throat. Thinking, "This is it," Gregory lay there motionless. Fear made its claim, it gripped him. Slowly speaking the words, "If it's money you want, you can have it. It's in my bag."

Slowly pulling the knife away, Gregory's assailant put it away. Retreating into the shadows, a voice said, "I don't want your money, I want your help."

Turning around to look, Gregory said, "That's a heck of a way to ask for help!"

Speaking from the bushes, the cry rang out, "Will you help me?"

"Step out into the light." Gregory insisted.

Slowly emerging from the shadows, an elderly Indian man appeared.

"That's not the way to make friends," Gregory joked nervously.

Asking the elderly man to share the fire with him, Gregory thought that would ease his apparently untrusting mind. As both men stared each other down, they sat down across from each other, only the flames separating the two.

"You've been following me, haven't you?" Gregory asked.

The Indian nodded his head in silence.

"You've from that reservation, aren't you?"

Breaking his silence, the elderly man said his name was Joe Yellow Hawk, Chief of the tribe. As Gregory listened, the chief told him why he was following him.

"There are very few of us left, but we have heard of the great power. Missionaries have shared their wisdom among us, but many of my people don't believe or trust the words of the white as I do."

Interrupting, Gregory said in an enthusiastic tone, "Go on, I'm listening." He didn't realize it was custom to never interrupt a Chief while he was speaking.

"Many of my people don't believe in the man named Jesus like I do. He lives within me and the great Spirit guides my way. Many call you Moses, that's why my people call you *One who walks with stick*. The hearts of my people are heavy, our troubles are many. That's why I ask for your help."

Pointing his finger to a group of trees, the Chief said, "I have one of our young men tied there."

Interrupting again, Gregory said, "Why'd you do that?"

The Chief went on to explain that the boy was possessed by evil spirits and had suffered with them for quite some time. The boy constantly cut himself and terrorized the tribe. Their medicine man tried to cure the boy, but failed. That's why the Chief decided to follow Gregory and ask for his help.

"Chief, why did you tie the boy up and bring him all this way?"

"Because he's my grandson."

"Why did you wait so long to tell me?" Gregory asked.

"The time needed to be right. The sign had to come. My people understand patience where others do not. The eagle has great meaning to us, it was the sign."

"You want me to help your grandson, don't you Chief?"

The Chief nodded his head yes.

Gregory instructed Chief Yellow Hawk to pray with him first, then bring the boy over to the fire where he was to untie his grandson. The Chief prayed in his native tongue while Gregory prayed in one other than his own.

After they finished praying, the Chief went over to the tree where his grandson was and untied him from the tree. The Chief led the boy over to the campfire where he sat him down and untied his hands. Laughing and swearing, the boy glared at Gregory through the flames.

Staring at the boy while his grandfather watched, Gregory commanded, "Name yourself, you foul spirit!"

As the boy laughed, a deep voice other than his own said, "We are many!"

Gregory stood from his sitting position and so did the boy while screaming profanity.

As Gregory stared at the boy, he said, "I say sit down, in the name of Jesus."

Still screaming profanity, the boy sat down. Placing one hand on the boy's forehead and the other on his neck, Gregory began to command the evil spirits out of him, one at a time. Although it took several hours, the boy was finally delivered from what possessed him. Every demon that dwelled within him had left. Gregory, as well as the Chief, knew that deliverance came not by their power, but by the power of a Savior.

The Chief and his grandson got a normal night's rest at last. The three ate breakfast in the morning after they woke, then shook hands and parted ways. God had once again demonstrated his enormous power, lives had been changed and the captive was set free.

Gregory left the Chief and his grandson at Little Salt Lake, but he didn't leave the sense of being watched there. That feeling followed him all the way to the town of *Enoch*. Gregory thought it was strange that he would enter a town that was named after a man he had read about the night before. Laying down his backpack, Gregory pulled out his Bible and refreshed his memory of Genesis Chapter 5 and Hebrews 11.

As he closed the book, he noticed someone sitting on top of a large rock just outside the town. It was a man who Gregory recognized, or so he thought. Walking up to the man, who appeared to be well up in years, Gregory looked up at him. Thinking it odd that he was up there, Gregory said, "Do I know you?" Staring, Gregory said, "I know you from somewhere, but I forget the name."

"Names are not important." The elderly man replied. "You have been reading Genesis and Hebrews, haven't you?" The man added.

Thinking it was odd that he knew that, Gregory said, "Now I remember, Echo Lake, the tournament, your name is Enoch!"

As soon as Gregory uttered those words, a glorious beam of light fell upon the man. "I am Enoch." He replied.

In fear, Gregory dropped to his knees as he whispered, "The real Enoch!"

"Tell me how to get close to God like you did." Gregory asked.

He answered by saying, "Walk in His ways," then he disappeared.

Gregory sensed he was on holy ground. His spirit broken, he placed his face in his hands and wept there for hours. The overwhelming feeling of the experience was with him for days. It consumed his very being from *New Harmony* to *Leeds* and beyond. He would experience quiet and solitude all the way to the Virginia River, then things would change.

Interstate 15 crossed the river at the Arizona state line, but there was a surprise waiting there. Cars were parked on both sides of the bridge. As Gregory walked across, many shouted, "Have a drink with us, Moses!" All of them appeared to be drunk. Some even followed Gregory in their cars as they drove on the side of the road at a snail's pace. In one of his journal entries, Gregory called it, "An embarrassing send off party,"

The Nevada state line was only ten miles or so from where Gregory crossed the bridge. He followed 15 as it cut across the northwest corner of Arizona, but he couldn't get rid of the drunken following. Being rude often, Gregory told them to get lost, but they were too intoxicated to understand that Gregory just wanted to be left alone. It took well into the evening, but the last of the following left him as he crossed the Nevada line.

Before making camp that evening, he wrote the following journal entry:

"October 15th."

"I crossed over into Nevada tonight, boy am I happy. I leave three hundred and fifty miles of Utah and Arizona behind me, but it took forty five days. It's getting colder at night now. People are starting to honk their horns and leave stuff at my camp. Some are even throwing things at me as they drive by. People! If that's the start of a following, I say no thanks!

Solid Rock

It didn't take Gregory very long to reach Glendale, Nevada, but unfortunately, it didn't take the media long either. Representatives from Larry King Live and other talk shows asked for an exclusive interview with Gregory, but he repeatedly said no. The hassle of people blocking his way was becoming constant.

Thinking about traveling at night to avoid the crowds once more, Gregory saw a large fire in the distance. As he approached it, he saw signs posted everywhere. They read, "<u>You're on Indian land</u>!" He thought to himself, "Great, I'm on another Indian reservation!" Gregory tried to leave by using one of the secondary roads, but that would prove to be difficult.

Standing at the end of the road were two men, they were waiting on Gregory. They were from the *Moapa* tribe and Gregory had trespassed on their land. They walked up to Gregory, then both men grabbed an arm each.

Pulling his arms away from them, Gregory said, "Listen here fellows, I don't want any trouble."

Grabbing his arms again, both men said, "You're *one who walks with stick.* Come with us."

Not happy about it, but knowing he was out numbered, Gregory went with the men. The large fire Gregory noticed from the road was a celebration

powwow the tribe was having. The men took
Gregory over to where the Chief was sitting.

"Have a seat!" The Chief said.

Gregory said, "Kidnapping's a crime you know,"
as he wrestled with the men, refusing to sit.

"So is trespassing, *One who walks with stick*."
The Chief replied. "Now sit!"

Reluctantly sitting, Gregory said, "You guys
aren't big on warm welcomes, are ya?"

"Chief Yellow Hawk told me how you cast the
evil spirits out of his grandson."

With a sarcastic attitude, Gregory said, "I guess
the beat of the drums came through the wires."

The Chief didn't think that comment was very
funny. With a stern look on his face, he said, "Joe
Yellow Hawk's my friend!"

"Your friend greeted me with the blade of a
knife, did he tell you that?"

"I wouldn't have trusted you either."

Trying to stand up, Gregory said, "I'm leaving,
you can't hold me against my will. I accidentally
stepped on your land, sorry!"

"We've been waiting for you Matthews. This
celebration we're having is one of victory."

With a puzzled look on his face, Gregory sat
back down.

"We watch the news too you know." Extending
his hand, the Chief introduced himself. "I'm Red
Storm, leader of these people."

Gregory thought he would stay an hour or so,
but he ended up spending the night. The people
were quite friendly, once he got to know them. He
danced with them around the fire that night as they

celebrated life. Sleeping under the stars with new found friends, Gregory had an enjoyable experience after all.

Passing *Dry Lake* by, Gregory made it to Route 93 before dark the following evening. Two teenagers, who were prone to gossip, saw Gregory walking along the road earlier in the day. They attended *The International*, a church in Las Vegas. Recognizing him as Moses, the man on the news, they went directly to their minister and told of his coming. Their minister dropped everything he was doing and ran out the door, much to their surprise.

Driving out to where Gregory was spotted, it didn't take the minister long to find him. The minister found the glow of Gregory's fire, parked his car, and walked into his camp.

Gregory responded by saying, "Whatever it is you want I'm not interested. I just want some sleep!"

Determined to meet this man, the minister extended his hand. Gregory shook it as the minister stared at him in silence.

Gregory said, "What?"

"Sorry ... I'm Bishop Paul. I pastor at *The International* in Vegas."

"What is it you want pastor? I'm really tired."

"I had a dream about you last night, Gregory. I have this tremendous need in my spirit to tell you about it, that's why I'm here!"

"How did you know I was here?" Gregory asked.

"People are talking, brother. I've seen your story on the news more than once myself. You're getting to be somewhat of a folk hero around here."

Leaning over to poke a stick in the fire, Gregory said, "You wanted to tell me about a dream?"

Bishop Paul sat down and told Gregory of his dream, but not all of it. The dream ended in Los Angeles and the Bishop felt it was best left for Gregory to experience, so he remained silent about how it ended.

"That's a good dream," Gregory replied.

"You're headed for Los Angeles, aren't you? Bishop Paul inquired.

"Get that from the dream too?" Gregory asked.

"No … from the news."

"That's right, I'm on a journey. I don't know what I'll find in L.A. though."

The Bishop knew Gregory was on a journey. He knew what would happen in Los Angeles, but he kept it to himself. Something was holding the Bishop back from revealing the entire vision.

"I have a good friend in Los Angeles. His name is Tom. He pastors in South Central. His church is called *The Dream*."

Bishop Paul knew God had something to do with this, but he didn't realize the extent of it. At the exact same time Bishop Paul had his dream, Pastor Tom had his. The dreams were identical, except for one thing. God gave Pastor Tom some final instructions.

"I'll give my friend a call," said the Bishop. "I think he wants to meet you."

"How will I know who he is when I get there?" Gregory asked.

"Oh, I'm sure he'll find you!"

Before Bishop Paul left, he told Gregory the church was having an outdoor concert on Friday night. He slid a ticket in Gregory's pocket; it was for a front row seat. Before driving away, Bishop Paul rolled down the window and said, "We'll see ya Friday night. God bless ya, brother!"

Gregory spent the following day dodging the dotted line of I -15. The sun being at a forty five degree angle to the horizon, he decided to make camp for the night. Shortly after he settled in Gregory made a fire, then he heard an explosion. At first it sounded fairly far away, but then he heard more and they started getting closer. Gregory didn't realize it, but he was on the Nellis Air Force Base gunnery range. Maybe he shouldn't have climbed through that hole in the fence back by the highway after all.

A spotter in an observation tower was watching the firing exercise when he noticed the faint glow of Gregory's fire. Using a set of powerful binoculars, the observer caught sight of the intruder. The Sergeant grabbed his radio, then yelled, "Stand down, cease fire! Cease fire!"

Watching the exercise from a bunker, the Base Commander heard the order to cease fire. A shout came over the airwaves when the Commander said, "Sergeant, this is Colonel Hughes. Why are you stopping the exercise?"

The Sergeant responded by saying, "Sir, we have a civilian on the range!"

Hughes then ordered his jeep to be brought up.

Gregory noticed the explosions had stopped, but other than that, he didn't give it much thought. He reasoned in his mind that it was just a demolition project or something. After all, he did see a lot of construction going on.

Gregory went back to enjoying the fire when he heard a couple of *clicks* behind him. He heard the words, "Turn around slowly!"

As he turned around, Gregory saw several M-16 rifle barrels pointing at him. As he raised his hands, more soldiers surrounded him, then a jeep pulled up. Stepping out of the jeep was a full bird Colonel. It was Hughes, the Base Commander. "Boy, you're in a whole lot of trouble!" The Colonel emphasized.

The Commander ordered the soldiers to search Gregory's belongings. After searching his backpack, one of the soldiers said, "He's clean, Sir," and handed Hughes the journal. The Colonel scanned through the journal, closed it, then began to stare at Gregory. "Do I know you young man?" The Commander asked.

"I don't think so." Gregory replied.

"Yes, I do know you. You're that guy who's been on the news. Moses … right?"

"My name's Gregory Matthews … not Moses!"

The Colonel ordered his men to put their weapons down. Extending his hand, the Commander said, "You're becoming quite a folk hero around these parts."

Gregory shook the Colonel's hand to say, "You're the second person in the last two days to tell me that."

The Commander asked Gregory how he got in there. He told him through a hole in the fence. "Show me that hole," was the Colonel's response.

After looking at the damaged fence, Hughes said, "This won't do." After much thought, the Commander said, "Well, Mr. Matthews, it looks like we have two choices here. We can either arrest you or let you go."

Gregory said, "I like the second choice best!"

The Colonel said, "I'm probably breaking regulations here, but it won't be the first time and I guess it won't be the last."

He ordered the soldiers to make camp around the damaged fence. "Mr. Matthews, it's too late to get anybody out here to repair that fence so we're going to guard the opening till dawn. I haven't bivouacked in a long time, may I join you?"

Surprised by the Commander's actions, Gregory said, "I would be delighted, Colonel."

Gregory Matthews, a common citizen, slept with those special-forces that evening. It was quite an honor for him. When the sun came up in the morning, the Commander told Gregory he was free to leave and he didn't waste much time getting out of there and back on the road.

Later on that day, Gregory saw the skyline of Las Vegas. Remembering Bishop Paul's invitation, Gregory pulled the concert ticket from his pocket. The church's address was printed on the ticket so Gregory followed the exit to his destination.

Once he got there, Gregory saw the large tent on the church's property, but he didn't see Bishop Paul. The concert wouldn't start for a while so Gregory made the best of the time by talking to the soundman and the roadies.

Bishop Paul did eventually arrive. He told Gregory his seat was right between him and his wife on the front row.

"I think you'll like tonight's entertainment, Gregory, it's DC Talk and 3rd Day."

Gregory was glad he came. He loved both groups, especially DC Talk. As Gregory sat through the concert, he thought the Praise and Worship tunes were electrifying. Bishop Paul knew the last song would be a special one for his friend, he planned it that way. He conveniently forgot to mention the surprise to Gregory beforehand.

At the end of the concert, DC Talk and 3rd Day both walked on stage. Grabbing the microphone, one of the singers said, "We have a special guest in attendance tonight, ladies and gentlemen."

Looking down at Gregory from the stage, they motioned him to come up.

Reluctantly doing so, Gregory walked on the stage.

Placing his arm around Gregory, the lead singer said, "This is Gregory Matthews. I'm sure you've all heard of him." The crowd roared.

Gregory sang the last song with them, but not very well. He was off key. To be quite honest, he couldn't have carried a tune in a bucket, but no one seemed to care though.

It soon came time for Gregory to leave and he said the usual good-byes, but that night was a night to remember. He got to attend a free concert, sit on the front row, sing a song on stage with the band, and even pose with them afterwards for photographs.

Gregory spent the evening sleeping in the desert on the outskirts of Vegas, but before falling asleep, he thanked the Creator for the evening. He simply said, "God, you sure are good!" He didn't realize it, but God wasn't quite finished yet.

Gregory made it as far as *Sloan* the next day. While he was making camp, he got interrupted by another Reporter. This time it was CBN. They wanted to run a story about him. He told them to come back later, after the journey.

While the two were talking, two large tour buses pulled to the side of the road and parked. Several people filed out of those buses and made their way over to Gregory and the Reporter. He recognized them as the band members of DC Talk and 3rd Day.

With a surprised look on his face, Gregory looked at the Reporter and the band members to say, "What's going on?"

The Reporter spoke up to say, "This is partly my fault. I had reservations in the same hotel that these guys did. I told them I knew where you were. I said I canceled my reservation, and that I was coming out here to spend the night with you." Smiling at Gregory, the Reporter said, "I guess they canceled theirs, too!"

As Gregory looked around, the band members nodded their heads in agreement.

"You don't mind … do you?" The Reporter asked of Gregory.

His response was, "Are you kidding?"

Everyone eventually settled in to enjoy the evening and the warmth of the fire, but because both bands were touring together, and they had to be in Phoenix by the next day, many fell asleep early. Morning would come early for the group.

Morning did indeed come early. When Gregory woke, everyone was gone. His new found friends slipped away in the middle of the night without waking him, but the memories did endure.

Before Gregory reached the California border, he decided to stop in the small town of *God Springs*. Gregory was never much of a coffee drinker before, but that had changed. The town had a coffee shop on the square like none other. Owned by Roger and Nancy Huff, *The Soul Coffee Shop* was a Christian Coffee House with an outstanding reputation.

As he stared at the hundreds of signed autographs and photos on the wall, it didn't take the owners long to recognize who Gregory was. He noticed that several big name artists had performed there, including the two he had just spent the previous night with.

Walking up to Gregory, Roger and Nancy asked for his autograph. "We would like to hang it on the wall with our collection," they said. Gregory stayed for a while then he got back out on the road. He reached the state line shortly there after.

Gregory wrote in his journal, "It's October 21st. I'm saying goodbye to Nevada today. Six more days are gone, and so are a hundred miles. I met a lot of nice people in that state, some were even rockers. I used to think badly of that kind, but I've changed my mind. They may play rock and roll, but it's the gospel they're spreading. I have to admire them for that!"

The Reward

Frustrated by the hot California sun, Gregory stood with raised hands as the sweat ran down his face. He cried out, "Okay, Lord, I'm burning up here! When are you gonna let me in on the plan? Why does everything have to be a big secret? You said come out here, well, when did you plan on telling me why?"

Gregory's thought to himself was, "There's not a drop of water or shade around here for miles. No wonder they call this God forsaken place *Ivanpath's Dry Lake*."

Pulling his Bible from the backpack, Gregory thought he would unfold it and put it on his head. Reasoning it would be better than no shade at all. When he opened the Bible, an acorn fell out of it. As he stood in wonder of how it got there, the desert sand quickly swallowed it up. Stepping back, Gregory witnessed a miracle right before his eyes. The acorn grew into a mature oak in a matter of minutes. Dropping to his knees, Gregory wept for what felt like hours. Hugging the tree, Gregory said, "Lord, I don't deserve a reward after the way I talked to you. I'm sorry. Thanks for the miracle of shade!"

In the cool of its shadow, Gregory made camp for the night. He thought to himself, "Boy, most of us just take these things for granted," as he laid down to sleep under that which God bore. When daylight broke, Gregory blessed that place, calling it *Holy Oaks* before he departed. He would never realize the significance of that prayer, but many in the area soon would. A lake sprung up there just days later, as did many oaks among grass. God created something miraculous there. Many would come to call it a desert oasis of impossibility, but others called it *Miracle in the Sand.*

It didn't take Gregory long to reach *Mountain Pass* as he considered its four thousand foot incline. As he made his way through its picturesque landscape, Gregory began to hear the crackle of engines. Several dirt bikes were riding along what the locals called Hell's Ridge. The riders didn't even realize Gregory was there, as they sped by.

Using the lower portion of the ridge as a ramp, many of the daredevils jumped the road to land on the other side. Two decided to take the safety of the low road, just barely missing a barbed wire fence that lay ahead. Bringing up the rear was the least experienced one of the bunch, Jake Watts, who had just learned to ride only three weeks before. His friends called him Spite, and the seventeen year old was about to ride into the unexplained.

Following his friends, Jake didn't see the fence until it was too late. His first reaction was to lay the bike down on its side, but that would prove to be costly. Gregory watched with fright as the bike slid under the fence with the rider still on it. The bottom strand of wire caught the boy under the chin, popping his helmet off. Gregory ran to where the rider fell, the horror of the sight was almost too much to take. Lying at the rider's feet was his motorcycle, still running. Gregory reached down to turn it off, then he saw a pool of blood forming under the boy's head.

As the boy lay on his back unconscious, Gregory stared at the deep cut across his throat. The injury was so severe it almost decapitated him. Gregory tried to hold the wound together with his fingers, but the boy's life was slowly flowing from Gregory's grip. In a panic, He shouted, "Stop! Oh … God … stop! In Jesus's name, I command you to stop!" Much to his surprise, Gregory watched as the blood stopped flowing through his fingers. After that, the boy's throat became extremely hot to the touch. So hot in fact, that Gregory had to remove his hand. Right before his eyes, Gregory witnessed another miracle.

As Gregory watched, the gash began to close on its own. Slowly working its way across the boy's throat, an invisible force removed any sign of damage. Feeling the boy's throat once again, Gregory noticed it was cool to the touch this time. Amazingly, there were no scars. It was as if nothing happened!

Regaining consciousness, the boy sat up. He asked Gregory who he was and what happened. Not knowing whether to tell him of the miracle, Gregory said, "You fell."

The boy asked, "Why'd you bring me back?"

Gregory replied, "I don't understand?"

Closing his eyes as he looked to the sky, the boy said, "I remember racing on my bike, then I was flying toward a bright light. When I got to the light,

I was standing with angels, thousands of them. Oh … it was so beautiful! Then I noticed where the light was coming from, it was Jesus. He told me I had to go back. I asked him why. He said, a servant commanded it.” Turning his head to look at Gregory, the boy said, “It was you, wasn’t it?

Gregory stared at the boy in silence. He didn’t understand what he had really done.

With a puzzled look, the boy said, “Why didn't you let me stay there? I don’t understand? Why'd you do that, mister?" Gregory could only stare at the boy in wonder. His mind filled with many questions he had no answer for.

It had taken the other riders a while to realize their friend was missing before they decided to double back. Jake later told his friends about his near death experience, but none of them believed him. Unable to explain the fresh pool of blood, just Jake and Gregory had faith in the tale.

Not far from *Halloran Springs,* the following day, Gregory was wandering a desert called The Mojave. Out of water and becoming quite thirsty, Gregory decided to rest on a large rock. When he placed his hand on the side of the rock he noticed it was damp. Looking down along the bottom of the massive boulder, he found a small crack. Flowing from the crack was a pretty steady stream of water. Cupping his hands, Gregory filled them for several drinks. As soon as Gregory satisfied his thirst he filled his canteen. Moments after he filled it, the water stopped flowing. Any moisture that remained quickly evaporated in the hot sun.

As he read from his Bible Gregory wanted to give thanks for the water, but he really wanted to see what the word had to say about the subject. Becoming quite emotional, Gregory felt God was speaking directly to him while he read Isaiah 58:11.

"The Lord will guide you always; he will satisfy your needs in a sun-scorched land and will strengthen your frame. You will be like a well-watered garden, like a spring whose waters never fail."

Walking away from that stone with such a sense of gratitude in his heart, Gregory struggled to define it with pen. Although a defining word rarely eluded him, Gregory had difficulty explaining the experience.

His growing frustration with the public did later reach a boiling point. He just wanted to finish the task quietly, but that was becoming impossible. He started writing in the margin of his journal: "I wish people would just leave me alone!" He discovered that as long as there were people, solitude was rare and it was becoming increasingly harder to find.

Intrusion of his camp by strangers now seemed to be a daily occurrence. He didn't mind if their cause was noble, but many of the interruptions weren't. Gregory had little patience for those who let selfish gain dominate their conversation, he simply asked them to leave. In some circles he was gaining celebrity status, but that wasn't something he cared for.

He wrote of admiration for the Christian bikers who spent the night with him near *Baker*, but he also wrote in the journal of his distaste for the art of sales.

"I'm really starting to dislike salesmen. I guess the manufacturers just can't resist the temptation. They keep sending their sales representatives out here to gain an endorsement. Everyone of them have a contract in hand, I always turn it down. <u>I don't care about any of that stuff, why can't they understand that?</u> It was tennis shoes in *Lenwood*, camping equipment in *Yerno*, and of all things at the *Cronese Dry Lakes*, fishing lures!"

Walking into *Victorville* some days later, Gregory would witness what could be best described as the ugly side of life. *Victorville* wasn't a big town, but then again it wasn't a small one either. Most of its forty thousand residents had worked at the only factory in town, but hard times forced it to close. Many of its employees lived from paycheck to paycheck, and it didn't take long for panic to set in.

As Gregory walked the downtown streets he could hear lots of yelling. He walked towards the noise, curious to find out what was going on. About the same time he got there, so did a policeman. It didn't take the cop long to recognize who Gregory was. He introduced himself and both men shook hands. As they stood across the street, Gregory asked, "What's going on over there? What's all that shouting about?"

"Well, lots of people lost their jobs when the factory closed. The economy isn't doin' so good around here now, and people are really gettin' worried!"

197

"But why are all those people standing in front of that church?" Gregory asked.

"It's the only one left. The rest of them had to close their doors. No money!" The cop replied.

Many were standing outside the church when its pastor walked out the front door with a bullhorn. Speaking through it, he said, "Members step forward. All others … we can't help ya!"

Things got quite ugly after that and tempers began to flare. Gregory noticed a woman standing in the crowd with her two small children. They were hanging on her legs, their faces were quite dirty. A man in the crowd yelled, "For God sakes … this is America!"

Another shouted, "I'm gonna lose my home!"

Many cried out, "We're hungry!"

A sickening feeling finally arrived at Gregory's stomach when a man screamed, "Damn you to hell, Reverend!"

As he turned to the cop, Gregory said, "This is unbelievable! What are you gonna do?"

The policeman looked down to say, "Pray," then he turned to walk away.

Gregory just couldn't leave there without doing something. He walked over to the town hall to ask for the mayor. Handing him all the money he had, Gregory told the mayor, "Here, feed your people!"

Gregory left there broke, but it didn't matter. He had made a difference in the lives of others, and that's what was all important.

Gregory made a stop at *Cajon Junction* the following day. It was there, at that crossroad, that God told Gregory of His plan, by way of a dream.

He revealed to Gregory that a retiring pastor was about to hand his church over. Gregory was instructed to accept the church because God told its pastor he was to do so. Gregory would become lifelong friends with the pastor, but he still didn't fully understand its meaning, the vision he would later call, "Inheriting a dream."

Walking along I-10, not far from *Upland*, Gregory saw the taillights of a passing car glow bright. The vehicle stopped, then began to back up. Gregory had no idea what the driver was trying to do, so he cautiously stood in the ditch. Backing to where Gregory stood, the driver pulled along side. The teen threw it into park as the gears of the transmission ground to a halt with a terrible sound.

Rolling down the passenger side window, the driver shouted, "Hey, you're that Moses dude, right?"

In no mood for conversation, Gregory started to walk away as he said, "Can't anybody remember my name?"

As Gregory walked away, the young man became determined. He made up his mind he was gonna talk to Gregory, no matter what. Gregory walked down the ditch as the driver slowly rode the burm along side. Shouting out the window, the teenager said, "Dude, I need to talk to you!"

Gregory waved his hands in silence, as to say I'm not interested and go away. Frustrated, the driver stopped his car. Trying to remember Gregory's real name, he finally did. Shouting out the window, he said, "Gregory Matthews! I got something to say!"

That got Gregory's attention; it stopped him in his tracks. With his back still to the vehicle he thought about turning around for a moment then did. Gregory walked up to the car, placed his hands on the top and leaned over to peer inside.

"What do you want, kid?"

"What is it with you adults? You never listen!"

"I'm listening … what do you want?"

Pulling a handful of money out of his pocket, the boy handed it to Gregory.

"What's this for?" Gregory asked.

"It's my paycheck."

As he tried to hand it back, Gregory said, "I can't take that!"

"If you'll just listen for a minute, I'll tell you why you have to take it." The boy explained.

Humbled, Gregory stood to listen. Holding his hand out, the boy shook Gregory's hand.

"I'm John, my friends call me *Shift*."

"Glad to meet you, John." was Gregory's response.

John went on to say, "I saw your story on the news a few weeks back, but I didn't think much about it until yesterday. I was in study hall, but I didn't have any homework so I started doodling on my notebook. I kept writing the word Moses for some reason. My study hall's last period, and after the bell rang I went to Bible study. It's a student run Bible class that's held after school on Tuesdays. As we were praying, the thought kept going through my mind, 'Give your all when you see him.' I had no idea what it meant until the Holy Spirit revealed

it as I passed ya. That's all the money I got! I'm
sure He knows you need it."

Gregory stood back; he was in awe of the
youngster. Tears began to well in his eyes.

"I got to go, I'll be late for work," John said.

Gregory just stood and stared at the boy and
then the money, he couldn't get over the boy's
obedience.

"Hey, I got an idea!" said John. "I work at the
Rite-Mart there in Upland, its only about a mile or
two from here. Stop by, I'll buy ya dinner. I work
at the snack bar. OK?"

"I should buy you dinner." Gregory replied.
"Besides, I thought you said that's all the money you
had."

Nodding his head, John said, "I got some friends
that owe me."

Putting his car into gear, John said, "Bye," as
slowly drove off.

Thinking he forgot to thank the teen, needing
supplies anyway, Gregory decided to stop at that
department store. Word must have spread fast
about Gregory because people were waiting for him
at the front door of the store. As soon as Gregory
arrived, somebody paged the manager. Gregory
signed a few autographs and then tried to fill his
shopping cart. He soon felt a tap on his shoulder.
When he turned around he noticed it was the store
manager.

Extending his hand, the manager said, "It's a
privilege to meet you, sir. I'm Gary, the Manager.
If you'll let us, we'd like to treat you to dinner … on
us!"

Gregory asked, "Did your employee, John, put you up to this?"

Playing dumb, the Manager said, "Why, I don't know what you're talking about."

Excepting the offer, Gregory and the Manager walked over to the snack bar while a small crowd watched. Gregory saw John working behind the counter and he thanked him for his kindness when he stepped to the front of the line. When the food was ready, Gregory and the Manager sat down to eat.

John told many of his friends Moses was in town. Gregory had a surprise waiting outside, a reward you might say, he just didn't know it. The Manager was in on the whole thing, but he never once spilled the beans.

When he finished his dinner Gregory shook the Manager's hand to say, "I got to fill my list then hit the road. Thanks for all that!"

The Manager just smiled. He knew there was oh so much more going on.

Gregory paid for his items then walked out the door. Much to his surprise several students were lying on cots in the parking lot. Once the students saw Gregory come out the door, they started yelling, "Hi!"

Walking over to where they were, Gregory looked down to ask, "What's this all about?"

The spokesperson of the group said, "It's a sleepover … fund raiser."

"Fund raiser for what?" Gregory asked.

"For you … Mr. Matthews!" They all replied.

Pointing to his chest, Gregory said, "For me?"

The spokesperson said, "Yes, it's all for you."

John's friends had come up with the idea, and the Manager gave it his blessing. The students asked Gregory to join them while many others began to file in, all with cots or sleeping bags in hand. Quite moved by the gesture, Gregory marveled as the lot slowly filled. It wasn't just students who were participating; adults were also getting in on the act. The students placed four blankets at each corner of the lot to accept donations. Being weighted down with generosity, the blankets became quite heavy with things like money, watches, jewelry, and even a few canned goods.

All the excitement didn't go unnoticed. Camera crews arrived to report on the phenomenon. Several miles away, Pastor Tom was watching the live broadcast from his Los Angeles home. Knowing what he had to do, Tom got his jacket on and told his wife he'd be back later, he was driving to *Upland*.

Arriving late that night, Pastor Tom couldn't believe what he saw. The entire parking lot was full of people. Some were sleeping on cots, some in sleeping bags, and others were just lying on a blanket. The crowd was estimated later at around five thousand.

After he arrived, Pastor Tom walked up to Gregory to introduce himself.

"You have a question for me, don't you?" Gregory asked.

"Why … yes … I do … but how did you know that?" Tom replied.

"He's been telling me."

"God's been telling me a few things, too." Tom said.

Gregory said, "I know what He's asked you to do, Tom." Nodding his head, Gregory said, "I'm ready!"

With a lump in his throat, Tom told Gregory of his decision to retire and asked if he would pastor his church. Gregory didn't have to think twice about it; he said yes.

Gregory looked at Tom and reassured him that he was doing the right thing. "The Lord told me you were to give the leadership of the church to me, Tom."

"I'm glad God told you too. I've been struggling with this decision ever since He told me to make it. I just didn't know who I was to hand *The Dream* over to … but now I do."

As he shook Gregory's hand shortly before leaving, Tom said, "I'll let you finish the course. When you get to L.A. give me a call."

Well, Gregory didn't have to worry about knowing God's plan any more. He didn't have to stand in the unemployment line either, but that didn't stop Satan from trying to trick him though. After Gregory left *Upland*, he got quite a few job offers. The first being for a sales manager's position in *Raging Waters*. That company specialized in bottled water. Another was for a Plant Manager position for a factory in *Baldwin*. But the best one was from a bank in *Rosemead*. The job was one of Vice-President. But in the end, Gregory said no thanks to them all. He knew what he was really called to do.

Gregory finally made it to *Los Angeles.* The journey had taken him exactly nine months, his rebirth you might say. It had covered a little over three thousand miles and fourteen states, five of those he crossed on the run. It had been a wild ride at times, but Gregory would soon come to realize the worth of it all.

He Took the San Bernardino Freeway to *Hayward Park*; Gregory arrived on December 4th. He didn't realize how big of a state California really was. It had taken him forty-five days to travel the nearly two hundred and seventy five miles.

When Gregory arrived at the Park, he gave Pastor Tom a call. Tom had just told his congregation of the decision the Sunday before. Although some were saddened by it, many were willing to welcome their new pastor with open arms. One of the members of the church board was the Manager of a television station there in Los Angeles. It was his idea to capture the turning of a page at Hayward Park. With Pastor Tom's consent, the Manager sent camera crews to the Park to capture the moment on tape.

Tom went to meet Gregory at the Park and the cameras were waiting. As Tom walked up to Gregory the cameraman was posed to catch it all. After all, Tom was a well known symbol of LA society and the cameraman didn't want to miss a thing. After the two men shook hands Tom turned to the camera and announced his retirement.

"I'm handing the church over to the watchful eye of Gregory Matthews. Some of you may know him as Moses," Tom chuckled.

Moments after Tom rewarded Gregory with the keys, someone yelled, "That's a wrap!"

Freedom

When Tom presented Gregory with the keys to *The Dream* many were watching, including "L." She stood on the street corner watching the event on the many television screens. The department store window was full of sets, and all were tuned to that station. With a tearful eye, she watched her father accept the presentation. Wiping a sleeve across her eyes, she made up her mind to pay the church a visit. She had become an undesirable though. Falling hopelessly into the gutter of sin, she thought, "Will he even be willing to see me?" She had never realized the true meaning of forgiveness before, but she was about to embrace it head on, along with the one who defines it.

Walking through the front door of the church the following day, "L" noticed someone else there. He was praying in front of the altar, and never heard "L" come in. It appeared they were the only two in the building. While he kneeled, with his back to the door, "L" quietly took a seat on the back row. While he prayed, for what seemed like hours, "L" grew impatient. She did then got out of her seat and walked to the front. Standing behind the person, she cleared her throat several times. When that didn't work, she tapped him on the shoulder. Much to her surprise, Gregory turned around.

Standing to hug his daughter, Gregory said, "Sweetheart, what are you doing here?"

"I saw you on television, Dad. I never figured you'd be a preacher!"

Gregory said, "Have a seat," as the two occupied the front pew.

With a tearful eye, "L" said, "Dad … Mom's dead."

Placing his hand on her shoulder, Gregory said, "I know, James told me. I'm so sorry Sweetheart!"

"Mom hired a lawyer to draw up the divorce papers after you left. Then she threw them in the trash. I dug em' out!"

Pulling the tattered decree from her coat, "L" threw it on the floor.

Thinking it best not to question her about why she carried those papers, Gregory continued to listen as he rubbed her shoulder. In the back of his mind, he knew why she did that. It was obvious that "L" had to have something to hold onto, Gregory could tell she hated the idea of a broken home.

"Dad, I got something I have to tell you."

"What is it Sweetheart?"

With a steady tearful stream now flowing down her cheek, "L" said: "After you left, I took a brush from the bathroom. Mom said she was gonna throw everything away you owned!"

With a shake of his head, Gregory said, "I don't understand Sweetheart."

"When you left, my friends kept teasing me. They said you weren't my real father, that's why you took off. I ignored it for a while, but then I had to do something about it, I needed to know. I was bound and determined to prove them wrong. I took some of your hair from that brush and had it tested." With a long sigh, "L" said, "Dad … you're not my father."

With a puzzled look, Gregory said, "What?"

"I paid for the DNA test with my allowance. I'm sorry, but I'm not your girl."

"L" leaned over to place her head in Gregory's lap, as he began to weep.

Clearing his throat as he rubbed the back of her neck, Gregory said, "You'll always be my girl!"

The two sat in silence for quite some time. "L" wiped her tears away, then cleared her throat to say, "There's more I have to tell you!" Sitting up in her seat, "L" looked at Gregory and went on to say, "Mom took an overdose the night after I told her about the test. She left a suicide note."

Pulling the torn paper from her pocket, "L" began to unfold the note.

Gregory asked, "Is that the note?"

"L" replied, "Yes," as she prepared to read it.

"Sweetheart, you don't have to do this!"

Looking down, "L" said: "I need to."

Gregory listened with a heavy heart as "L" read her mother's suicide note.

"Dear "L,"

"I'm sorry to leave you like this, but I have failed as a mother. Forgive me. Believe me; I thought he was the father. I guess I've been living a lie all these years. I was a poor excuse for a wife, and that's something I will never be able to make right. I had a lot of problems, but there was no excuse for

never showing you two love, I was wrong. Don't make the same mistakes I did."

"Be a good girl, Mommy loves you!"

Leaning over, Gregory put his face in his hands and began to weep at length.

Placing her hand on Gregory's shoulder, "L" said: "I'm sorry … but there's more!"

After a few moments, Gregory raised his head to look at "L."

"Dad … Grandpa said I had to live with him, he got a court order. I didn't wanna live with him. I wanted to live with you, that's why I ran away. James said you were on your way to L.A. so I hitchhiked here. I thought I could be a movie star or something!"

Hanging her head in shame, "L" said, "You know something, Dad? The streets are a scary place!" Momentarily hesitating, "L" went on to say, "I ran out of money, then I got cold and hungry. I didn't have any place to stay so I slept on the streets."

With streams of mascara running down her face, "L" told Gregory she was a hooker.

Leaning over to place her head in his lap once more, "L" said: "I'm so ashamed. I didn't think you'd see me. What am I gonna do, Dad?"

"Do you want me to help you, Sweetheart?"

Looking to Gregory with open delight, she said, "I'd like that!"

Gregory said, "If you're ready to change your life, I'd like to introduce you to someone!"

"I don't wanna go back to the streets, Dad!"

Gregory asked, "Will you pray with me then?"

"I don't think I've ever prayed before," was her response.

Standing from their seats, both walked to the altar. As they knelt, Gregory said, "Sweetheart, have you ever heard of a guy named Jesus?"

"L" nodded her head yes.

"He's the only one that can truly forgive you of sin. If you're really serious, I want you to repeat this prayer after me, ok?"

"L" nodded her head again. "L" seemed to be transformed after she repeated that sinner's prayer, her face shined with an immaculate glow.

As they embraced each other, both still crying, Gregory said, "All's forgiven, Sweetheart. You will never be the same!"

With a smile, "L" asked, "Can I stay with you, Dad?"

Hugging her a little harder, Gregory said, "Of course you can!"

After a few moments, they sat down again. In the midst of lighter conversation, "L" said: "Say Dad … Mom never did tell me what my name meant. Why don't you tell me."

"What would you like it to be, Sweetheart?"

Detecting a sense of reluctance in his voice, "L" said, "Well, I've always liked the name Laura!"

"How'd you know that's what it was?" Gregory asked.

"Lucky guess?" "L" reluctantly replied.

"It sure was! From now on we'll call you Laura, ok?"

"L" knew Gregory was hiding something, but she didn't pursue the definition. She never once brought

the subject up again. She continued to call him
Dad, but never referred to herself as "L" anymore.
Moving in with Gregory Laura began to adapt to her
new environment, one of a normal teen.

The church owned a beautiful parsonage just
down the street, Gregory and Laura now called it
home. Gregory was reading in the den shortly after
they settled in. He spent a lot of time in that room,
the one he called *The Study*. While Gregory
prepared for the up-coming Sunday service,
memories of Becky began to fill his mind.
Succumbing to a heart of curiosity, Gregory picked
up the phone to dial the operator.

"Operator … May I help you?"

"Can I have information for Broken Arrow,
Oklahoma." Gregory asked with a nervous tone.

"Yes … Can I help you?"

"Do you have a listing for Henry Stover?"

A moment later the Operator said: "No Sir …
There's no listing for a Henry Stover. There's one
Stover listed for Broken Arrow. That's Ruth Stover
on Main. Would you like to try that?"

"That's it!"

"It's 968-555-1862."

Gregory said, "Thank you," as he hung up.

Gregory sat for a moment in silence then dialed
the number with trembling hand.

Gregory was thinking, "Oh boy, it's ringing,"
then he became surprised by the sound of a familiar
"Hello" on the line.

"Ruth?" Gregory asked.

"Yes."

"It's Gregory Matthews."

"Oh … Greg. How are you?"

"I'm doing good. How's Henry doing?"

Pausing for a moment, Ruth said, "He's gone, Greg. He passed away last year."

"I'm sorry to hear that."

"Don't be. He was quite ready. He's in a much better place than you or I now."

"I'm sure he is."

"So … Greg. Why are you calling?" Ruth asked.

"Well … to be honest … I've been thinking about Becky."

"You have?"

"How is she?" Gregory asked.

"Well, she's a teacher at the Broken Arrow Jr. High."

"Is she married?"

"No, she never got married."

"Is she happy?"

"I don't know, Greg. Maybe you should ask her."

"Is she home?"

"No, she's not home right now."

Gregory cleared his throat to say, "Ruth … I'm sorry. I know I hurt your family, I apologize."

There was a vast moment of silence.

He tried again. "Ruth … I was wrong. I'm asking for your forgiveness."

A tearful stream began to flow down Ruth's cheek.

"Greg, we have always loved you, we never stopped. I know Becky was hurt, but she never stopped loving you either."

Tears began to well up within Gregory, too. Overcome by emotion, Gregory said, "I need to go … tell Becky I called."

Ruth said, "Bye, son."

Gregory hung the phone up and placed his face in his hands. With his elbows on the desk, he soaked its maple finish with a flow of tears.

After crying for quite some time, Gregory regained his composure. He leaned over to the computer and turned it on. The repetitive sound of: "You've got mail!" continued to echo from the screen. Annoyed, Gregory slapped the gray box and much to his surprise it stopped. As he read the only email, Gregory began to cry once more.

"Greg, It's Dad. I saw your story on the news. I've been following the papers, too. I looked up the church's web site, and decided to throw caution to the wind and write. I was wrong to treat you the way I did. I started drinking after you left. I dove in the bottle, the hard stuff. I was even homeless for a while. I'm sorry, Son. Forgive me for the fool I was. Dad."

Gregory replied by simply saying, "All is forgiven, Dad!"

A miracle bloomed forth in Gregory's heart that day. He was at last set free from that debt of hate he had for his Father. Finally pardoned from that prison of resentment, he was a captive no more. The torment of his thoughts no longer plagued him. He began to live in liberty. He began to walk in freedom. He forgave.

The Way

Startled by the sound of breaking glass, Gregory rushed to the living room. Staring through the broken pane, he saw several individuals standing in the street. Shouting obscenities, they dared Gregory to come outside. Gregory noticed a rock lying on the floor. Tied to the rock was a note. Gregory picked the rock up and untied the string that held the note on. The note said, "F*** you, Moses!"

Praying to himself, Gregory said, "Lord, protect me. Give me strength to strike down this attack," then he walked outside.

Hearing the disturbance, the neighbors had already called the police. Listening to a scanner, a television crew was only a block away when the call rang out. Thinking they could capture a police brutality incident on tape, they parked across the street and hid in the bushes. The Reporter and Cameraman lay in wait in hope of a breaking story for the nightly news.

Waiting in the street were several members of a gang. Standing at the head of the pack was their leader. Repeatedly flicking his lighter on and off and shouting obscenities the leader taunted Gregory. With a tremendous boldness, Gregory walked up to the leader and got within a few inches of his face. Soon surrounded by the others, Gregory was encircled by trouble.

Doing all the talking, the leader said, "They say you're a prophet. Prove it Moses. Walk on water!" As the gang laughed, the leader went on to say, "This is our turf!" Pointing his finger in Gregory's face, he said, "I tell you what to do!"   Flicking his lighter on, the leader held it in front of Gregory's face. "We're gonna burn your church down, Moses!" Again, the crowd laughed.

As the news crew watched, the Reporter asked the Cameraman, "Are you gettin' this?"

His reply was, "Yeah, this is gonna get ugly."

Gregory thought, "Lord, help me. I'm in trouble!" Then for some unknown reason, he had the sudden impulse to yell, "Repent! For the kingdom of heaven is at hand!"

That infuriated the gang's leader. Without warning, the leader pulled back his fist and swung at Gregory with everything he had.

In a blink of an eye, Gregory braced for the impact by closing his eyes. He thought, "This is gonna hurt!"

Immediately, the leader started screaming obscenities along with, "You broke my hand!"

But how could that be?   Gregory didn't feel a thing.

As he opened his eyes, Gregory saw the gangbanger standing in front of him holding his bleeding hand.

Across the street, the news crew watched in amazement. The Reporter looked at the Cameraman to say, "Did you see that?"

When the gangbanger swung at Gregory he hit something, but it wasn't Gregory's face. Captured on tape, his fist hit an invisible wall with such impact that it broke his hand and cut his knuckles wide open.

With extreme anger the leader yelled, "Kill him!"

As the gang drew close to Gregory, many pulled knives. Immediately they began to cover their faces. They screamed, "The light! Don't kill us!" As he just stood there, Gregory couldn't figure out why they were doing that. Neither could the news crew that was filming it all. Although Gregory, the Reporter and Cameraman didn't see it, the gang did. Standing behind Gregory were several angels armed with swords. The intense glow of their presence blinded the gang and they ran away when the angels drew their swords.

The Cameraman stopped filming after they ran away. When he laid the camera down he told the Reporter, "I've never seen anything like that before in my life. I'd say you got your story!" Jumping into their truck, they headed back to the station to process the tape.

Shortly after the gangbangers ran from the scene, the police arrived.

Stepping out of the squad car, a policeman said, "What's going on here? We had a report of a disturbance."

Gregory replied, "Oh, it's nothing officer … Just some kids."

Opening the door to climb back in the car, the officer said, "Ok, then."

Gregory quickly said, "See you at church Sunday?"

The officer climbed into the seat of the squad car, shut the door, and buckled his seatbelt. As he slowly inched the car forward, he rolled the window down and nodded his head to say, "Yeah, I think you will."

Gregory stood and smiled as the officer drove off.

The Reporter ran the story that evening on the nightly news. He began his report by saying, "I'm reporting the unexplained." The television station showed that tape over and over again. It became somewhat of a novelty. So much so, the mayor of Los Angeles couldn't resist the political opportunity in it all. He announced that the up-coming Sunday would be "Gregory Matthews Day" in L.A. Gregory didn't like all the attention, but there was little he could do about it.

As Gregory wrote his sermon on Saturday, he became overcome by the presence of God's Spirit. God said, "My son, write my book."

Gregory responded by saying, "What would I write about, Lord?"

"Tell of my glory that sustained thee," was His response.

"An autobiography?" Gregory asked. "It sure would be a boring one, Lord. Besides, I turned that newspaper guy down on a book deal already!" Laughing, Gregory said, "I can see it now, *The Bored and the Cross*. That sure would be some title, wouldn't it?"

A sense of urgency to write plagued Gregory's mind from that day forward. The feeling didn't leave him until he began to write the story. Quite

pleased by the obedience, God began to ease
Gregory's mind and stimulate his thoughts.

Sunday morning finally arrived and Gregory
was quite nervous about it. It was his first service
and he didn't know what to expect. Several camera
crews were waiting outside in earnest. Many were
hoping for an interview at the conclusion of the
service.

Running late, Gregory didn't have time to meet
the people as they filed in upon arrival. Entering
from the rear of the building, Gregory walked onto
the platform. Quite surprised by what he saw, tears
began to well in his eyes.

His inherited congregation was still intact, none
had left. Scattered among them were several
distinguished guests. Scanning the crowd, Gregory
saw the men in blue standing along the back wall.
L.A.P.D. had arrived in impressive style. Standing
with them was FBI agent Larry Winn, who gave a
wink.

Becoming progressively more emotional,
Gregory recognized many along the back row. The
mayor of Grand Junction was in attendance, he flew
in just for the service. Elvis Jones, his old
roommate from ORU was there, he was now a pop
star. Jim Smith was also there. He was the
homeless man who Gregory once ignored on Wall
Street. Dressed in a suit, Jim was no longer
homeless. He started a new business and was doing
quite well. Gregory noticed someone sitting with
his head down. It was the toll booth operator from
the Holland Tunnel, his guilt had led him there. He
cheated Gregory out of that hundred dollars, but he

later repented of that. At the end of the service, he dropped two hundred dollars in the offering plate. Also sitting in the back was Sara, the Reporter from Missouri who Gregory had encountered at a flea market. A news crew of one, she made the trip for personal reasons. She, too, was about to write a book called *His Miracles*!

The tears of joy began to flow steadily down his cheek as the audience began to applaud. Sitting in the center of the crowd were folks like, Lisa, the store clerk from New Jersey. Gregory had led her to the Lord in a coffee shop. John and Julie, the now debt- free dairy farmers from Pennsylvania. Mabelle, the woman with a heart for truckers. Gene and his wife Linda. He survived the heart attack that killed him, thanks to God's miracle. Wilbur and Mary Sutton, the campground owners who showed such kindness. Jim, his wife and son Billy, the father and son who interrupted their day of fishing to return that which was lost. As the boy waved, Gregory could not forget the memory of them.

Several of Gregory's dear and close friends sat on the front row along with many others. Sitting on the right side of the sanctuary were Lynn and David Linton, the youth pastors from Harrisburg. Pastor Peter from Basking Ridge, and even T. James Bradley, the evangelist. Forever touched by their lives, Gregory considered them sweet servants of God.

On the left side of the sanctuary sat John and his boss. Because they showed tremendous compassion for others, they were elected Rite-Mart's employees of the year. Ann Shore, the nurse from Illinois, was sitting with her husband Ralph. Sitting with them was the Hispanic lady and her baby that Gregory helped deliver. The Shores learned Spanish and became the godparents of the child. Next to them sat the parents of Katie Lynn Rogers. Gregory cried the most when he saw them. Sitting on the end of the row were James, Gregory's best friend, and Angela's father.

Sitting on the platform behind him, Laura gave Gregory a thumb's up when he looked at her. After he regained his composure, Gregory began his sermon. Preaching on love and forgiveness, his message lasted a little over an hour. When it came time for the altar call, many came forward. Gregory recognized the two standing in front of the rest. Angela's dad and James were the first in line for prayer, and Gregory prayed for James first. James whispered in Gregory's ear, "Please forgive me!" Crying, Gregory hugged James to say, "You're my best friend!"

Next to be prayed for was Angela's Dad. Gregory didn't know what to expect from him, he knew he had a heart full of pride. Before Gregory could lay his hands on him, he pulled papers out of his coat. As Gregory watched, he tore them into little pieces, threw them on the floor and grabbed him. As they hugged each other, he whispered in Gregory's ear, "Those were the custody papers for "L." I was wrong … I'm sorry. I loved money more than I did family. I was a fool. It took losing someone I love to realize that. I don't want to make that same mistake again. Can you and "L" ever forgive me?"

Crying harder, Gregory hugged his father-in-law and told him, "Love covers it all!"

As the service was about to conclude, the back doors of the church flew open. Everyone turned to see who it was. Gregory's father walked through the doors. He ran to the front and fell upon his face in front of Gregory and began to weep. Leaning down, Gregory fell to his knees. Picking his father up, both began to hug each other. Tearful streams of sorrow ran down Ed Matthews' face as he told his son he was sorry and that he loved him. Quite overwhelmed by it all, Gregory didn't realize he had impacted so many.

After the conclusion of the service, Gregory consented to a couple of interviews, but he had something more important and pressing on his mind. Telling the news crew he had something to do, he asked them to follow him over to the church sign. A box of letters was lying beneath the sign and the news crew taped Gregory as he installed them. Curious, everyone present watched as Gregory spelled out his message. It read, "Becky, I love you! I've been a fool, please forgive me. Will you marry me?"

Applause rose from the crowd while the news crew filmed the event. Someone shouted, "We're live!"

Miraculous as it may seem, Becky was watching the broadcast on Channel 2 in Oklahoma.
Overcome by joy, Becky began to cry. Shouting to

her mother in the other room, Becky said, "Mom, I got something I have to do!"

"What is it, Sweetheart?" Her mother replied.

"I'm goin' to L.A."

www.ingramcontent.com/pod-product-compliance
Lightning Source LLC
Chambersburg PA
CBHW072121300726

48975CB00003B/877